Sniffing Out Murder

LAYERS OF MYSTERY
BOOK ONE

LEANNE BAKER

Sniffing Out Murder

Chapter One

When I finally put Mojave in the rearview mirror, my grip on the steering wheel began to loosen. California City would be next, but I wouldn't relax until Highway 14 and Highway 395 merged in Pearsonville. There wasn't much to see in Pearsonville but derelict cars, abandoned homes, and someone's half-hearted attempt at resurrecting a ghost town tourist attraction around a general store.

Still, I welcomed it. Here, I could breathe. I inhaled deeply, savoring the faint smell of dust. It wasn't LA smog. Now I could unwind. Entering the Owens Valley in eastern California meant that I was only a little over two hours away from home.

Bishop. It was the weekend after Memorial Day and the Bishop Mule Days parade, races, competitions, and rodeo. Mule Days beckoned equine enthusiasts from all over the nation during this weekend. The population in the area ballooned toward twenty thousand campers. But with Mule Days over for this year, Bishop's population shrank to its normal 3,800.

Home. But it wasn't *my* home. The house in Los Angeles I owned with Blaine had been sold. I was heading back to where I'd been raised, where my parents still lived. After ten years of returning only for visits, I knew this was the right move. I needed to be around family, people who loved and supported me. This time was for healing, then building. I hoped to make a new life in my birthplace. Bishop, California, is a small town nestled in the Owens Valley at 4,151 feet above sea level. The surrounding rural High Desert area, bordered by the Sierra Nevada mountain range to the west and the White Mountains to the east, accounted for another two thousand residents. Tourism kept the financial lifeblood pumping. Fishing, hiking, and camping in the summer, then winter sports, including skiing and snowboarding at nearby Mammoth Mountain Ski Area, a mere forty-three miles north and 3,729 feet higher at 7,880 feet.

Fighting the highway hypnosis, I slipped off the cruise control to slow through the town of Lone Pine. An hour south of Bishop, the shadows from craggy Mount Whitney told me the afternoon was marching on. As soon as the speed limit lifted at the city limits, I pushed my foot on the gas pedal. I wanted to get to Bishop before dark. My parents lived in the McLaren area, west of the city limits and far beyond any streetlights. Dad was an inveterate remodeler. Every time I visited, there was a new driveway, lawn, or planter bed. Parking by memory in the dark was never a good idea.

What lay ahead for me? I had a line on a job doing the same work I'd done down south—court reporting for the City of Los Angeles. My application for the Inyo County Courthouse in Bishop was in progress. Until the county completed my background check and I got a written job offer, I'd help at my cousin's new bakery.

Opening a bakery in competition with world-famous Boulangerie was a tricky enterprise. I knew people in LA who drove the four and a half hours just to buy Boulangerie French bread. A little challenge wouldn't faze my cousin, Melody, or anyone else in my family.

Usually, this drive filled me with excitement to see my family, but as I passed through Independence, the Inyo County seat, I had to acknowledge my unhappiness. Today, I returned to stay with my parents for the foreseeable future, a loser, a divorcée, an unwanted woman. Dumped at age thirty-six. I felt like my life was over. I glanced in the mirror at the beginnings of feet near my eyes. I'm too young for them. Not bad looking by today's standards—brown eyes, oval face, and I stood five foot eight with a trim physique. I wasn't particularly athletic, but I stayed active. But now a solo act.

It would be an oversimplification to blame it all on Blaine. Still, he's the one who took my heart and trampled it to bits. He's the man I'd married, who promised love and honor for the rest of our days. The husband who broke those vows. The jerk who got custody of my dog.

Rusty was a big, goofy golden retriever/Irish setter mix. I missed him terribly. He'd kept me sane in the past months. He gave me a reason to get up every morning, to get out in the world. In the end, I loved him more than Blaine, which is why my ex-husband took him. I swear, my heart was more broken over the loss of Rusty than Blaine.

The desert floor lay before me. This was the outer edge of the Great Basin—the High Desert and a hostile terrain. I remembered a sixth-grade field trip into the desert that lay at our family's back door. Five generations ago, it was a fertile agricultural basin, irrigated by the generous melting Sierra snowpack. When the Los Angeles Department of Water and Power diverted its water in 1913, the Owens Valley went from fertile to fallow. Farms dried up, soil blowing away in storms of dust. The plants that grew here now had evolved into a stubborn spikiness of built-in defenses. With plant names such as tarweed, snakeweed, fleabane, and stinkweed, as well as sagebrush and rabbitbrush, the Owens Valley wasn't welcoming for everyone.

To a city person, this country might seem harsh and uninviting. Not to me. I rolled my window down and let the breeze blow through my light brown, shoulder-length hair. The wind smelled like home, and a little like tarweed. The heat of the late spring day was peaking, eighty-five degrees on my car display. The screen didn't display the lack of humidity. June humidity averaged thirty percent, enough to keep my Southern California frizzies at bay. In an hour, it would cool down gradually, so nights were pleasant, if not cold, at this time of year.

Bishop was an island in the desert, isolated from the metropolitan areas of Reno to the north and Los Angeles to the south. Not everyone who moved to this mountain paradise was able to tolerate it. California Highway Patrol and L.A. Department of Water and Power wives often found shopping at the local Kmart sadly lacking. And the nearest Macy's store was over three and a half hours away—one way. It wasn't for everyone.

Shadows of the Eastern Sierra mountain range crept across the valley floor. The small town of Big Pine was behind me as I pushed north. Another remarkable landmark in this striking landscape, the Caltech Owens Valley Radio Observatory, appeared on my right. For miles and miles, nothing taller than scrub and a wayward cottonwood obstructed the view. Then, just past Big Pine, huge satellite dishes appeared on the desert floor. Locally nicknamed the "Ears", was a set of six telescopes used by astronomers to track radio sources in the sky. The atmosphere here was so clear that this location was optimum for the study of astronomical science. Locals joked about the "Ears" listening for alien conversation.

Wilkerson lay ahead to the left of Highway 395, a tiny collection of small homes and trailers nestled against the western base of the mountains.

I'd better hurry if I wanted to make Bishop before dark. This time of year, that meant being in town by 8:45 p.m. Pressing on the gas pedal, I glanced down to be sure my headlights were still on as a safety measure. Head-on collisions weren't unusual on this four-lane highway. Drivers often exceeded the speed limit because the road sat straight and visible for many miles in most places. It was easy to get complacent.

Headlights were on. I looked up.

Luminous eyes glowed at me from the roadway as I barreled toward them. Coyote? No. A dog?

It didn't matter. I stomped on the brakes. Thank God no cars were behind me. No one was around at all, except for the animal who limped off the asphalt.

Did I hit it? I replayed the seconds before the stop. No. I didn't feel or hear anything.

Letting the adrenaline play itself out of my system, I pulled my car over to the shoulder and opened the door. I saw the canine's ears bouncing above the sagebrush in an odd, uneven gait. Injured for sure, he headed up a slight slope toward Wilkerson.

Going home? I didn't know how injured he was. In the dusky gloom, I saw quarter-sized blood droplets on the pavement. The thought of leaving didn't sit right with me. If it was an injured coyote, it could be dangerous. I would need to call the authorities.

The distance between the road and the first line of homes in Wilkerson was about a half mile. I'd dressed comfortably for driving, in jeans and a T-shirt, and thankful with the choice of tennis shoes rather than my usual sandals.

It was 8:10 p.m., and dusk was upon this part of the desert.

I made the decision quicker than it took to tell. I pulled across the highway lanes and onto a shoulder facing south. I wanted to walk this area to see if I could find the animal. Armed with the car keys, I grabbed my cell phone, then closed and locked the car. I found a game trail and headed for the first house with lights on.

Chapter Two

Shadows deepened across the sandy valley floor as I wended my way up the gradual slope toward Wilkerson. The small community of five hundred sat on a low ridge between an eastern escarpment of the Sierra mountains. When last I visited, there had been one paved road and the side streets of dirt and gravel. It wasn't a town, but more of a valley oasis that became a neighborhood. Desert scents of rabbitbrush and sagebrush drifted on the evening breeze. Distant cottonwood trees lining Rawson Creek whispered a sweet song. Brushing by the pungently sweet scrub, I turned on my phone's flashlight to avoid obstacles like the desk-sized rocks and thorny brush. I kept an eye out for snakes that might be slithering to a night's rest.

The silence was profound. After years in Southern California, the lack of constant traffic noise required some getting used to. I thought it funny how a person can adapt to the hustle of the world, then be shocked at its absence. My ears pricked for the sound of an animal limping ahead of me, but I heard only the gentle wind in the trees.

A sense of solitude engulfed me. Suddenly, I recalled my father warning me not to stray too far from civilization. A tingle of fear crept up my spine. Bishop school-aged kids had grown up hearing stories of prospectors swallowed up by the desert and tourists who wandered off the trails to never be seen again. The desert can be disorienting, especially if you don't know the mountains. But I did. Round Mountain loomed in the Sierras dead ahead.

Hoping to find the injured animal, I let the few dots of lights from houses guide me forward as I followed the beam of my phone.

A yelp, like from an injured dog, pierced the night. It sounded like it came from the south to the left of my path. I veered off the trail toward it, being careful to look over my shoulder at the house lights in Wilkerson. Must keep my bearings. Hurrying my pace, I decided against calling for the animal. I didn't know what lay ahead.

I heard a man's voice, raised in alarm. Then a car door slammed, and the quiet engine of an electric vehicle turned over. Tires scrabbled on the dirt road near the houses. Thinking the sounds might be related, I shifted my direction toward where the yelp came from.

For the second time tonight, my nerves were rattled. I stopped and switched off the flash. A white coupe raced along the asphalt road out of Wilkerson. Even in the deepening night, the driver hadn't turned on the headlights.

There was something wrong out here. The driver hadn't wanted to be seen. And the animal was hurt.

As the road noise faded, I turned on the flashlight

and walked on. The dog was silent now, no sound of movement, no yelping.

By my estimation, I walked another hundred feet when I heard the breathing.

I stopped, taking in the sound. Human or animal? I couldn't tell. The road was less than ten feet away.

It was all I could do to work up a whisper. "Hello? Are you okay?"

A whimper came in answer.

I waited. Okay, no attack was a good thing. The animal knew I was here and didn't have the energy or resolve to strike. "I'm here to help you." I said in a low, soothing tone as I walked toward the sound.

Another whimper.

My flashlight revealed the dog, a beautiful, full-grown German shepherd by the look of him. Appearing well-fed, nevertheless, stickers and weeds clung to his coat. He'd been in the desert for a little while. Now, he sat on his haunches in the sand as if guarding something. A small gash on his shoulder oozed blood.

A low growl rumbled through his chest. "Whoa, pooch." The dog needed help, and this was more than I could handle alone. Turning off the flashlight, I checked reception. No bars. I'd have to get back to the car to make the call. But first, I wanted to see what he was guarding. I hoped it wasn't another injured animal.

I backed up two steps and sidled around to his rear, speaking softly, trying to reassure him. He kept his eyes on me. Expecting to see another injured animal, I looked beyond him and saw a leg. A human leg. A female. Not moving.

My instinct to go to the person to check for signs of life was tempered quickly by another ominous growl.

It was too far to return to the car. I backed away,

circled a bush, and finding a path, made for the nearest house with a light on. The young woman who answered the door must have thought there was a lunatic on her steps.

"There's a woman out there," I pointed in the general direction. "She's down on the dirt, not moving. There's a big dog guarding her, and he's hurt too. Call 911." When the woman reached for her landline, I turned to go back. She was making the call.

A minute later, her voice screeched over the distance. "The ambulance wants you to show them where she is."

"I'll meet them here." I signaled where I'd be, at the end of the dirt road past the last house. The woman and the dog were so close to the road. I knew the ambulance would probably take ten minutes. I'd hear the siren from miles away. I had a thought—if the woman was alive, she'd surely need help. Maybe I could use this time to lure the dog from protecting the woman. Or better yet, get him to trust me.

I shouted at the woman standing on her doorstep, "Could I get a bowl of water for the dog?"

Four minutes later, I slid the bowl of water across the sand toward the dog, getting as close to him as I dared. He glanced at the bowl, then back to me, then settled in the sand. He was there for the long haul.

Food might work. The woman was still on her doorstep. I hollered, and she disappeared into her house. A minute later, she trotted toward me, a patty of ground beef in her fist. After a quick glance over my shoulder, she retreated.

This might do the trick.

It did.

I pulled off a piece of the meat and tossed it at him.

At first, he seemed to ignore it. Then he nosed around it, and it was gone.

His ears perked. Within seconds, I, too, heard the sirens. Help was on the way.

I tossed another knot of meat to him, this time closer to me. I kept an eye on him, trying to see if the woman was breathing. From where I stood, she looked still. I couldn't get closer to help her, but getting control of the dog now became my task. Slowly, I petted his head, then softly grabbed the nape of his neck. No collar. I'll call him Fido.

By the time the ambulance turned onto the street, they'd switched off the siren. In their headlights, I hoped they'd see me with my grip on the dog's nape. I rose to a high crouch, one hand on the dog, the other waving them down. The unit pulled up to the edge of the road thirty feet from me.

While exiting the ambulance, the young, beefy driver made eye contact with me and saw Fido. He slowed a fraction, long enough for me to yell across the sagebrush. "Do you have a rope or leash or something to secure this dog?"

The wary driver reached behind his seat and tossed me a length of rope. It was looped, lasso fashion, and had a D-Clip at one end. Perfect.

To the dog, my hands smelled—and tasted, I'm sure —of hamburger. I held my breath that he wouldn't take a bite to see. But he acted compliant enough to let me clip the rope around his neck.

Pointing behind me, I shouted, "She's about thirty feet in that direction. I'm not sure if she's breathing. I couldn't get close enough…"

The ambulance driver and his slender partner approached, needing to pass me to get to the patient. A deep bark erupted from the dog. I tightened my grip on the rope as he lunged at them. "Hold it, Fido. They're friends." Almost falling backward, it took all my strength to hold him. The two men sprinted past us and were soon swallowed up in the darkness.

Growling, the dog pulled me after them. We stood five feet closer to the medics, who were now speaking to each other in muted tones. Both had flashlights, one on his ball cap, illuminating the gloom.

Fido kept pulling toward them. I looped the rope around my hand, wishing the cops would show up to help me control this animal.

Three feet closer. Fido's pointy snout growled and snapped at the men as they worked on the woman. He was only two feet away from them.

Over his shoulder, the medic yelled, "You got that dog under control, lady?"

I couldn't answer. Another foot, and we were almost on top of them. I grabbed a handful of stubborn sage-brush to anchor us. The dog, tense, quieted—still focused on the woman.

The medics had turned her over to work on her. In the glaring, unnatural light, I saw her face.

Oh no. It felt like someone had punched me in the stomach.

The woman was Melody. My cousin.

Chapter Three

I groaned as I dropped to a nearby rock. How I managed to keep my grip on the dog, I'll never know. He'd stopped trying to get to the medics, which was a blessing, and although he focused on them, he sat beside me. Every now and then, a whine escaped, but I barely heard them. The medics seemed to realize that I knew their patient and hurried to prep her for transport. As they strapped her onto a backboard, a glimmer of hope that she was still alive fanned inside me. I stood and pulled Fido out of their way. They stopped in front of me, and the skinny medic asked, "Do you know this person?"

"Yes. She's my cousin, Melody Charters."

Wrestling with myself, I decided not to ask if she would be okay as they hurried past me. I didn't want to know. I had to keep the flicker of chance alive. They loaded her in the ambulance, and the siren faded as it disappeared into the darkness on its way to Northern Inyo Hospital. It was 9:00 p.m.

Melody was my friend as well as my cousin. She was one of the reasons I came back to Bishop. She needed my help with her burgeoning business, the bakery she'd named Layers. I think she was insightful enough to know I needed to get away from Los Angeles, to remove myself from Blaine and the effects of our sordid divorce. Away from the whispers and wary glances that reeked of shunning. We had friends, but it seemed movie people stuck together, and I wasn't one of them.

I'd told Melody that I didn't know anything about baking, but I could keep records accurately for a business, and even wait on customers. She'd told me she'd do the flour mixing, and I'd keep track of the dollar signs. She'd done it for six months without my help, but thank God, business was good enough that she needed me now.

God. Oh. I'd better call her husband and tell him. No, Wednesday evenings were Bible study sessions at Wesley's church. According to my aunt, Melody's mother, the members were often so enthusiastic that it wasn't unusual for sessions to go over time limits. It was a schedule no one messed with. Least of all, Pastor Wesley.

I couldn't call him. I couldn't tell him this news over the phone. I had to go to the church and tell him face-to-face. If Melody was alive, she was in serious condition.

Fido sat beside me, as obedient as a trained K-9. What to do with him? I couldn't leave him. I didn't want to wait for the sheriff. The ambulance driver threw me a roll of gauze for Fido's wound and said the cops would arrive as soon as they could.

I knew better. Having been raised in Bishop, I knew that delays in emergency calls were commonplace. Response time inside the city limits was more reasonable as they had less territory to cover. The Inyo County sheriff patrolled the second largest county in the state, with each on-duty deputy responsible for hundreds of square miles. From Mount Whitney to Death Valley, Inyo covered the highest to the lowest geographical points in the continental US.

No, I wasn't going to wait. I'd call my mother with an excuse to tell her I'd be delayed. She'd worry otherwise. Then, I'd see Wesley. Then I would call someone to take Fido to the vet.

Chapter Four

Wesley's New Life Fellowship Church was situated on North Sierra Highway, which extended from Main Street. It sat in a busy strip mall a block from the edge of town. When I drove into the lot, all the lights were off inside. I'd missed him. I didn't even get out of the car, I turned and headed south toward Wilkerson again.

Fido stayed in the car when I reached Wesley and Melody's home on the south side of Wilkerson. The dog barked like mad when I closed the door, but it didn't matter. He had to stay put. Wesley and Melody had a pair of cats, and I didn't know how the two would get along with a dog. I just hoped Fido wouldn't eat my upholstery.

The house was a small post-World War II ranch-style home. The garage had been converted into a family room in Melody's expectation of children who had yet to make an appearance. Sagebrush covered the yard while Wesley's car sat in the driveway, tic-tic-ticking.

The front door opened after my knock. Wesley

started, a shade of irritation crossing his face. "Sarah, this is a surprise. I..."

"Wesley, there's been an... an incident. Melody is injured, badly, I think. She's been taken to Northern Inyo. You need to get right over there."

He hesitated, eyes widening as the news sunk in slowly. He turned away, then wheeled around in a circle, patting his pockets for car keys. He shouldn't be driving. "I'll take you to the hospital and call Melody's dad."

Minutes later, he leaned on the passenger side of my car while I moved Fido to the back seat. I didn't want him to bark, or worse yet, bleed all over Wesley. I needn't have bothered. The dog sat quietly, and the bleeding had stopped thanks to the gauze from the medics. His head jerked from Wesley to me as we got into the car.

"What happened?"

"I don't know." My stomach flipped, recalling the scene. I nodded to Fido. "I thought this dog had been hit on the highway, so I followed him up to Wilkerson. When I caught up with him, he was guarding someone lying on the ground. It wasn't until the ambulance got there that I was able to see it was Melody."

"On the ground? She was on the ground?" He looked at me in earnest. "She is deathly afraid of scorpions and snakes. She wouldn't be there voluntarily."

I didn't want to be the one to tell him that she could be dead. The possibility tore a hole in my heart. I wouldn't do the same to Wesley unnecessarily. I wasn't a medical professional. I'd leave it to them. "I'll call Tom and have him meet you at the hospital."

"Sensible Sarah. Thanks for taking control." Wesley's face sagged. "Oh, God. Melody wasn't home when I got back from Bible study. I figured she was out for a walk with Jake or something. Oh, God, why didn't I go look for her?"

Ignoring the 'sensible Sarah' comment, I had no answers. I didn't know who Jake was, but it didn't matter. It might not have made any difference if Wesley had gone searching, but I couldn't tell him that. Feeling powerless, I called his father-in-law Tom's number. Thankfully, Tom was home and jumped to help his daughter and son-in-law. I concentrated on my driving, the dirt road, then the highway to the hospital. Wilkerson didn't have streetlights, and the highway was equally dark until we got into town.

The rest of the way, Wesley stared out the windshield, with an occasional groan.

When we arrived, I parked and went around to his side to open the door. He seemed incapable of doing it himself. He stepped out, then turned to me. "You're not coming in?"

"No, this dog's injury needs attention, and there's no one on duty at the shelter. I'm going to take him to the vet." I reached out to put a hand on his forearm. "But I'll be there as soon as I can."

Tom's gray pickup sped into the emergency room parking lot, screeching to a halt. A tall, lean, rancher-type, burnished by the sun and seen often in the valley, he hopped out of the truck. Beside us, when we walked through the sliding doors, he fired questions faster than I could answer.

"Tom." I tugged on his sleeve to get his attention. "Melody is inside. They have the answers you're looking for."

He grimaced, "Okay."

Ever the man of action, I had to pull harder on his

sleeve for him to slow down. "Will you take Wesley in and stay with him? He's not functioning very well."

The cowboy hat dipped with his nod. Now, he had a purpose.

"I'll be back as soon as I can."

Chapter Five

The North Sierra Veterinary Clinic was on Highway
395 on the way out of town, past Highway 6,
which branched off at the Wye and went all the way to
Maine. I knew the clinic was closed, but like most, there
should be an emergency number to call. Parked in front, I
tried to recall the layout. It had been years since I had
been up at this northernmost part of town. The injury
had stopped bleeding, and he probably needed a piddle
break, but I was reluctant to get Fido out of the car with
only a rope tied around his neck. There wasn't much traffic, but I'd hate for him to get loose.

I punched in the emergency number and thankfully got
an answer right away. The vet, Burl Vancleef, asked a few
terse questions and, after my answers, said he was on his
way. Fifteen minutes later, a red pickup drove up. The
driver, a middle-aged man with a handlebar mustache,
got out to open the gate, then parked inside. He returned

to secure the gate, and in five minutes, I was inside with Fido.

Vancleef was more than happy to let Fido out for a break in the fenced area. We stood by the back door as Fido sniffed and piddled. "You say you found him on the highway?" In Bishop, "the highway" was Highway 395 unless otherwise specified.

I nodded. "Wandering in the road, then he ran up the hill toward Wilkerson. I—I found him just outside the houses." It was time to get Fido inside to be checked out. "Come here, boy."

"Bring him in here, exam room B. I'll see if he has a microchip." The room was the size of a large closet with steps of various heights. Vancleef led Fido to the lowest one and began the exam. He felt between his shoulder blades, nodded with a grunt then left the room to find the microchip reader. Moments later, I heard an exasperated cuss. Then from another room, the same, only louder. He came back into the room, scowling. "We have a new vet tech, and she's rearranged everything. Any chance you can bring him in tomorrow? We'll have it in hand by then."

"I planned on taking him to the shelter tomorrow." I felt oddly distressed at the thought.

"I bet they know where their reader is." Vancleef shrugged. He put a light muzzle on the dog and told me to hold his head. Fido put up no resistance. He must've had a muzzle on before. Vancleef loaded Fido in his arms and placed him on a higher step. The movement was so fast and graceful that the dog didn't have time to protest.

The vet pulled out a stethoscope. "Let's take a look at this big boy." Heartbeat, lung sounds, and temperature—the exam took a few minutes. Vancleef happily pronounced Fido in good shape except for the injury.

Then, Vancleef unwound the poorly applied gauze, tsking at the job.

I volunteered, "That's my fault. The gauze is all I had."

"Well, it did the trick, didn't it? There's a gash here that needs to be cleaned up. No stitches, though." Fido fidgeted as Vancleef palpated around the wound. Using cotton gauze and antiseptic, he cleaned off the blood, then gave a loud grunt of disgust. "There are slivers of wood in this wound."

"Wood?" I wondered how wood…

"Yeah, someone hit this dog." Vancleef sighed. "This isn't from rolling around in the desert. There's no other material, other than weeds and stickers, on his coat. I'm going to take pictures of this for a cruelty case if you find who did this."

Holding back the giant hug I was going to give Fido very carefully, I marveled at the cruelty we can visit upon each other, and our animals.

"People…" the vet began but couldn't finish. He sprayed something on the injury and bandaged it. "I'll keep the slivers for evidence if the abuser is ever caught." He stroked Fido's head. "It's a dang shame to hurt any animal, but this guy…"

I felt my throat thicken as I pictured someone striking this dog.

"I'll have to shave the hair around it so a bandage will adhere." He looked at me intently. "Can you hold him?"

"Sure." While Vancleef left to get the shaver, I wrapped my arms around Fido. As if he knew I needed comfort rather than him, the dog laid his head on my shoulder. My heart melted. "What a good boy you are."

Vancleef must've heard me because when he returned, he smiled broadly. "He surely is a nice dog. You got lucky with this rescue. He could've been a jerk." He reached into his jeans pocket. "I found a collar that will do for now." He handed over a lightweight blue nylon collar.

"What happens to him now?" I grimaced, dreading his answer.

Vancleef smiled. "You could take him home. Come back tomorrow when we find our microchip reader. We'll contact the owner and hopefully return this good boy to his home." He reached over and scratched below Fido's ear. The dog leaned into him affectionately.

"Or..."

The vet shrugged. "...Or we can keep him here. The shelter will pick him up in the morning and figure out what to do with him."

Words failed me as I thought about him in a shelter. I shook my head.

Chapter Six

I called Mom on the way back to the hospital. She'd already heard that Melody was injured but didn't know any more. I told her the basics about Fido and asked if he could stay the night in my room. In her typically understanding manner, she said, "Of course. Drop him off here if you want, but you need to get to the hospital."

Dread grabbed my insides. She was right. But I didn't want to take the time to make the trip home then the hospital. "Thanks, but I'll keep him with me. I'm on my way there now." Sensible Sarah. I'd fought that tag all my adult years. Sensible is a synonym for boring.

Fido laid down in the back seat when I got out of the car at the hospital. The sheriff's deputy met me at the emergency entrance. The medics had pointed me out when I arrived. Having worked in the courts, I knew a great many police officers. With all different personalities, most reflected their community. I was grateful that a badge never intimidated me. That was of little consequence when I recognized this deputy as the neighbor down the street from my aunt's house. He was the burly kid who always got a bloody nose when hanging upside down on the monkey bars at school. Kelly McSorley, who still sported a butch haircut, the same cut as in school. He was the kid who never went to the dances because he had to work on his uncle's ranch. I'd always felt sorry for him.

"Hey, Sarah."

"Kelly." This wasn't the place to catch up or talk about old times. "Melody?"

Kelly took off his cowboy hat and gripped it across his chest. I braced myself for the worst. "She's gone, Sarah. I'm so sorry."

The finality of it settled on me. Melody was gone. My worst suspicions came true. I dropped to a nearby chair and took a moment to gather my emotions. There were others who were even more devastated than I.

"Wesley and Tom?"

He nodded and replaced his hat. He was all business now. "They're inside. Wait." He reached out and laid a hand on my forearm as I started down the hall. "I need to ask you some questions."

"Now? Can't it wait?"

"No, it can't." His broad face twisted into a grimace as he pulled out a notebook and pen. "The medics tell me you found her. Is that right?"

Holding in my impatience, I reminded myself he had a job to do. I'd listened to cops outline the process of their investigations in the courtroom more times than I could count. The sooner he had answers, the quicker he could find whoever was responsible. "Yes." I recounted the episode, from seeing the dog on the highway until I watched the car speed away.

"What kind of car was it?"

"I couldn't see. It was dark." I looked over his shoulder to see if I could determine which room Wesley and Tom were in. The emergency room was to the left, a darkened hallway off to the right. They could be anywhere.

"Could you tell if it was a sedan or an SUV?"

"Too small to be an SUV. A sedan, I think."

"What color?"

"I don't remember."

"Was it dark or light?"

"Kelly, I told you I didn't get a good look. Why d'you keep asking questions?"

"People remember a lot more when they're asked specific questions." He sighed, unhappily resigned to making me uncomfortable. "Please, Sarah."

"Light, it was light. Probably not white, but I couldn't be sure."

"Anything else noticeable about it—like dents, a trailer, a roof rack, something like that."

"No, nothing." In a room down the hall, a light switched on, providing enough light to see an open door halfway down. Maybe they were inside. "No, wait." I had to get this right. My information would make a difference. "A roof rack, I think." Trying to picture it, my recollection was of a kind of frame on top, which looked like antlers. "Like a rack for a kayak."

"That's good, Sarah. This really helps." For the first time, I met his gaze. He'd been patient with me, and I appreciated it. He glanced out the door, and he froze.

Sheriff Stan Dorsey filled the entire doorway as he arrived. In a showy uniform with medals dotting his big chest, his round face radiated goodwill. It felt oddly inappropriate to me. The faint smile that didn't extend to his eyes put me on edge. I'd never met him as he was from a south county family.

Dorsey swept off his tan cowboy hat while his beady eyes scanned the room. After a nod to Kelly, the sheriff's booming voice greeted the intake clerk at the counter, waving like he was on the campaign trail. He must have been. "Maybelle."

The woman's face held no expression. Not even a greeting.

"Where are they?"

"Twelve-A."

Dorsey sauntered to Kelly and corralled him to a corner, away from me. I imagined Kelly filled in the sheriff, answering in hushed tones. Kelly nodded to the open door. The sheriff straightened with what looked like indignation.

"Do what I tell you!" he snapped at Kelly, loud enough to turn the head of a woman waiting across the room. "Arrest or detain, I don't care." Dorsey pointed an index finger at Kelly's chest, then tapped it, hard. "Take him to jail."

"But," Kelly sputtered, about to defend himself. "I have a witness..."

"No buts. It's always the husband in these cases. Now, go."

"Sir, there was a car seen leaving the scene."

"Okay, link the car to the husband." Dorsey shoved Kelly toward the hallway. "Now go."

I couldn't believe my ears. It sounded like the sheriff told Kelly to arrest Wesley. I watched Kelly slink to the room. Moments later, Wesley's protests filled the lobby, and Tom's pleas echoed in the hall.

I watched Dorsey. Surely Wesley and Tom's objections would have some effect on the man. My indignation level rose with Wesley and Tom's as Dorsey moved back to the intake desk to watch. I didn't know what Wesley had told Kelly before I got there, but I was sure it wasn't an admission of responsibility.

The snick of handcuffs cut through my disbelief. Wesley walked out, hands secured behind his back. Tom followed, dumbstruck, and stopped beside me. As Wesley passed through the lobby, he met my gaze and shook his head. I knew he couldn't have hurt Melody. Tom must have agreed with me. This was all wrong.

Kelly steered his prisoner through the sliding door and out to his patrol car. Tom stood silent as he watched his son-in-law on his way to jail for Melody's death. From across the lobby, Dorsey said in his big voice, "Another crime solved. Score one for the good guys."

I turned and left before I said something I'd regret.

Chapter Seven

"Sarah, you must be exhausted." Mom hung my jacket on a hook by the front door.

"I am, but I'm running on nervous energy now."

Tall and elegant, even in the middle of the night, my mother looked around and asked, "Where's the dog?"

"He's in the car right now. I wanted to be sure you were still awake before I brought him in."

"Go get him." She shooed me out like a first grader.

I parked in the half-circle driveway in front of my parents' home. The vet had given me a nylon collar for Fido, the kind vets use for clients without collars. Now I had better control as he jumped out of the car. I walked behind him, letting him sniff for just the right place to relieve himself. As I watched Fido's excellent manners, my feelings of imposition on my parents relaxed. He sufficiently watered a juniper as I looked over the exterior of our home. McLaren home lots were one-acre minimum, but often more. It was country property with many homes keeping horses in their yards. With no streetlights, residents had to illuminate their own land. Dad had sodium vapor lights at the barn in the back, but the front was lit up like Disneyland with clear incandescent lights on posts.

The house was a single-story 1960s ranch-style home, ever popular in the suburbs, even though this was far from any metro area. Dad had the exterior painted since I last visited. With his meticulous attention, it was the prettiest, best kept in the neighborhood. Neither parent went in for tchotchkes, preferring the natural beauty of the mountain valley and desert surroundings. Mom loved flowers, but she kept the front yard natural with low-growing junipers, sages, and several varieties of buckwheat. Snowmelt drained into West Bishop ditches and passed through the backyard. It was normally used for irrigation and livestock, but in recent years, a drought had diminished the flow. The Murrays' water dried up late in the spring.

Mom met us at the front door, smiling at Fido as we ambled in. She greeted him quietly, making slow moves. "Oh, he's hurt." Mom knelt by Fido and looked him over. "Who bandaged him?"

"Vancleef at North Sierra Vet Clinic. I had to call him out."

"Thank goodness he's been seen and treated. Good work, honey. Come sit with me for a while. I have a pot of coffee on." She patted my arm. Fido looked up expectantly at her, his tail in a tentative wag. She extended a hand. Mom reached her fingers under his ear and scratched gently. Fido mouthed, licking and chewing. "He obeys so politely on a lead. He's been well trained."

"Right? Watch." I stood next to Fido and said, "Sit." I don't know much about dog training, but when an animal does what you tell him, when you tell him, that sounds like good training to me. "Someone put time into him and took loving care of this guy. The vet said he's microchipped but couldn't find their reader."

I trailed Mom into the kitchen. It was a bright, spacious room with wall-to-ceiling white cabinetry. The sink sat below a window overlooking the backyard, and past our property, to the north end of the valley, was an expansive cattle lease with the mountains to the left. An island divided the room from kitchen to dining area. Mom did most of her prep work at the marble-topped island.

"You'll take him to the shelter tomorrow?" Over coffee at the kitchen table, Mom's brows knit with concern. "You know Buster's been gone for almost a month now. It's so quiet around here without him." Buster was Dad's cattle dog, a loyal scrapper who only paid attention to my father. Both Mom and Dad were heartbroken at his sudden passing from a rattlesnake bite. I knew she was noodling around the idea of keeping Fido.

I blew out an exasperated breath. "He's growing on me, for sure. I wish I could keep him. But like I said, someone put a lot of effort into this dog. I'm sure he's missed."

She waved a hand, signaling the end of that conversation. "Tell me what's going on. If this involves my family, I want to know."

I filled her in, up until I got to the hospital. I couldn't just blurt that out. So much had happened in the past—I glanced at the time on my phone screen—five hours. The really essential information I held onto. "Where's Dad?" I asked, sipping the hot coffee.

"He's over at Anna's, waiting for Tom and Wesley." My father had grown close to Mom's brother over the years. The two men were like brothers in blood rather than law.

I held my breath for a second. I couldn't wait for them to be together. "Melody has passed away."

Mom slumped in her chair, covering her face. She stifled a sob, and her eyes were red when she finally looked at me. "How awful. What a waste of a beautiful young soul."

I nodded, knowing that there were no words to comfort her.

"Does Tom know?"

"He was at the hospital. But it gets worse. Wesley was arrested for her murder."

"Murder? It wasn't an accident?"

"I don't know the circumstances. I found her in the desert..."

"You found her?" Mom gasped. "How horrible." She reached out to my hand to comfort me, knowing how devastating it would be to find my dear cousin injured. A hug would come soon, but for now, the story I told was more important.

"Yes, just outside of Wilkerson, lying in the sand. About thirty feet from her house. Fido was standing guard over her and bared his teeth when I tried to get close. I had to con him with food from a neighbor and tie a rope around his neck so the medics could pick up Melody." I shuddered at the recollection.

Mom stood and reached a reassuring arm around my shoulders. "It must've been awful, honey."

"Much worse for others. Mom, I don't believe Wesley is responsible for her death. When I told him she was in the hospital, he went white as a ghost. You can't fake that."

Mom shook her head, agreeing. She stood, pulled open the freezer, and pulled out a hunk of frozen meat.

"I don't even know how she died." Fido nosed my hand, so I stroked his soft fur. His big brown eyes bore into mine. "There was blood on the sand when the medics picked her up but…"

"Does it matter? I mean, really." She stuck the meat in the microwave. "We need to concentrate on the living."

Mom had a point. Tom and Anna would be shattered. Melody was their only child and the light of their lives. I was glad Dad was with them. If I knew her, Mom would be on her way over when she had baked, cooked, or otherwise concocted something for the family. My mother was exceptionally suited to render comfort at times like these. She had a gift of knowing when to be there and when to be absent.

She also knew mourners would besiege Tom's house tomorrow. They were a well-respected family in the Owens Valley. Everyone would bring food, so the family wouldn't have to worry about cooking, but that was tomorrow. Tonight, my mother was already on a mission. She'd have a breakfast casserole ready to eat in an hour. I suspected another one would appear tomorrow.

Food. I glanced at my phone. It was just past two in the morning. I hadn't eaten lunch or dinner, and it dawned on me how hungry I was. Fido was probably just as hungry *and* thirsty. I sipped more of my coffee and asked Mom if she'd tossed Buster's food.

She shook her head. "Didn't have the stomach for it yet." I followed her directions and found an open kibble bag in the laundry room. Food and water bowls sat nearby. Fido had followed me eagerly. He whined enthusiastically when he saw the food. I put the kibble before him, he ate so fast that I thought he'd choke. He drank deeply, then nosed the leftover kibble.

He was done. My turn.

Chapter Eight

While making a turkey sandwich, I slipped from one side of the counter to the other. Dodging Mom while she was at work in the kitchen brought back strong memories. Growing up, Mom was always in the kitchen, often baking for a church potluck, a welcome dish for new neighbors, or some friend in need. I often thought the reason she kept so trim even after eating all that food was because she burned off so many calories making it. She moved with a graceful economy of motion that kept me in awe. Gray strands at the temples highlighted her light-brown hair, tonight pulled back in a sloppy ponytail. Deep pools of perceptive hazel eyes settled on those fortunate enough to have her attention. Her round face defied wrinkles, even after spending her life in the desert. One would never know gardening was her hobby. Strong and sturdy from helping several times a year at Tom and Anna's ranch, she had tanned to a light brown.

I gulped down the last bite and reached for my cold cup of coffee, wishing I could get to the coffee pot for a warm-up. Mom was like a whirling dervish in the kitchen but always efficient. "The bakery! Melody hired an assistant, didn't she?"

Mom stopped, drawing a wrist across her brow to sweep away an errant whisp of hair. "Oh my gosh. Thank goodness you remembered." She turned, giving me her full attention. "Yes, she hired Libby, Grant's little girl." Grant was a widowed neighbor—he lived between our house and Tom and Anna's place. I'd met Libby, but she was a child when I last saw her. I felt the stretch of time —I'd been gone a full ten years. Libby would be seventeenish. I thought.

Layers would be closed, at least for a few days, until we figured out what to do. But Libby would have to be notified. I needed to put a "closed until further notice" sign on the door. I hoped Libby had keys.

Now, should I wait until Libby wakes up? That would be about four in the morning if the bakers began at four-thirty. I glanced at the kitchen clock. Two hours. Should I try to catnap? No way. I couldn't sleep. Not with all that's happened. I looked out the window but couldn't see if Grant's lights were on.

I dredged my memory and recalled what I could about the Grant Armstrong family. Libby was an only child to Grant and Norrie. The Armstrong parents both worked for Med-Equipment, a local medical equipment supplier in the Owens Valley. Grant managed the business while Norrie took care of the office for scheduling, equipment, and insurance claims. A year or so after I moved south, I remember hearing about Norrie dying from a fall. There had been whispers about internal theft from the business, but Mom had quickly put a damper on such rumors. Poor Libby had enough pain to deal with in her young life.

I made my way to the coffee maker. Mom was elbow-deep in flour and frying up some country sausage.

Brunch Eggs

- *12 eggs*
- *½ cup melted butter*
- *½ cup flour*
- *1 lb. shredded cheese (jack or three-cheese blend recommended)*
- *1 pint cottage cheese*
- *1 tsp. baking powder*
- *1 tsp. salt*
- *1 lb. cooked crumbled breakfast sausage*
- *1 small can diced (mild) chiles*

1. *Mix all liquids with flour in a blender. Put the rest in a greased 13x9" pan, add liquids, and stir.*
2. *Bake at 350 degrees for 1 hour, loosely covered with foil.*

Now was the time to make a fresh pot. What would happen to the bakery, Layers? With Wesley in jail, who would make the decisions? Tom and Anna, maybe? My own position was far from guaranteed.

Melody knew I was coming home and why. She also knew the county was considering me for the court reporter job. She'd asked if I could manage the bakery with an emphasis on doing the books until I started my new job. I'd readily agreed as Melody and I were close. She'd hoped I could buy her time before she had to break down and actually hire a person to do the books. It felt like just the right activity to distract me enough from my divorce drama. Plus, I'd help my cousin.

I poured a cup of coffee for Mom and one for myself and sat at the table, watching Mom at work. Deft fingers plopped eggs, melted butter, and flour in a blender. She gave it a whirl. In a greased 9x13" pan, she'd laid shredded jack cheese, a layer of cottage cheese, baking powder, and salt. She poured a small can of medium hot diced green chiles and the crumbles of browned sausage on top. She poured the blender mix into the pan and stirred it all together. "There," she said with satisfaction after closing the oven door. "This will be done in an hour."

Stuffed French Toast

- *10 slices of bread*
- *2 packages of 8-ounce cream cheese, cubed*
- *12 eggs*
- *½ cup maple syrup*
- *2 cups milk*

Prep the night before:

Cut crusts off bread and cube. Place in a 9×13" greased baking dish. Next, sprinkle the cubes of cream cheese over the bread evenly. In a separate bowl, beat eggs, milk, and maple syrup together. Pour egg mixture over the bread layer, making sure to pour evenly. Cover and refrigerate overnight.

Day of eating:

Bake at 350 for 45 minutes and serve with additional warm maple syrup to pour over top.

Fido's soft breathing beside my chair completed the homey scene. There was no denying that I was growing attached to this dog. In my parents' home, watching my mother putting together a culinary masterpiece, a sweet dog beside me—all these things would've made me happy except for the reason it was happening.

Melody's death would be a loss to the entire community. Especially with Wesley incarcerated for her murder. This was so much more than an interrupted bakery business, or even a churchman being held responsible for his wife's death. Wesley had a position in the community, both religious and civic. Melody sat on the school board of the elementary district where she'd previously taught. They had people and family who loved them both, including myself.

I stood, suddenly gripped with a need to breathe fresh air. Fido at my side, I slipped out the door. "I'll be back in a few minutes." I said to Mom over my shoulder.

The fragrance of sagebrush, rabbitbrush, and the desert flora calmed me almost as much as Mom had hours before. A gentle breeze blew across my face, stirring the cottonwoods near the creek. A coyote yipped in the distance. The knots in my stomach loosened. Fido found a juniper to water.

Digging up memories of years past, I thought of how Melody had been more of a sister than a cousin. We'd been together all through elementary and high school— Wesley, Melody, and me. When Wesley went away for college and then seminary, Melody missed him terribly but knuckled down and got her degree in elementary education. They got married when he was ordained, and together they spent a year in Tacoma, Washington. Then a posting in Bishop enabled them to return. She'd finished her education during this time and gotten her teaching credential at Washington State. Melody had been so excited to return to her beloved hometown with her husband. They moved into a rental home in affordable Wilkerson. During the several months waiting for her California license to arrive, she got a job at a bakery in Mammoth Lakes, a resort town forty-two miles north. She came to love the bakery and the comforting smell of baking bread. She enjoyed the six years she taught but opening a bakery soon replaced teaching as her new dream.

Layers had been open a mere six months when she asked me to take over the bookkeeping and accounts. We'd been on the phone with each other during my breakup, so she knew my plans to return to Bishop. Many times, I said a prayer of thanks to God for giving me this thoughtful and compassionate young woman as a cousin and friend.

Now she was gone, and Wesley was in jail for her murder. Did he do it? And how could the sheriff arrest him without even listening to the only witness's account?

Melody wouldn't stand for Wesley's arrest. She wouldn't believe it. She'd fight for her husband's innocence. As I would. I owed her that, at least. Besides being my dearest friend, she gave me the hope and encouragement to move past my disastrous marriage.

But what if he *did* murder her? An accidental fall, fear of judgment from the community, the definite end of his ministry career all could have contributed to an unwise decision to leave. No, that couldn't be. I had to talk to him.

I looked up at the night sky, the stars were brighter here than they ever were in Los Angeles. No hint of dawn yet. Grant's house was still dark. I couldn't visit Wesley for several hours. I had plenty to do but couldn't get started until I saw Libby was up—another hour. I sighed, tired but amped from the events of the night and the coffee. No way could I get any sleep.

Fido had stayed by my side without a leash, watchful and obedient. I stroked his neck as we walked back into the kitchen. I poured myself a cup of coffee while Mom slid a casserole pan into the oven. She adjusted the timer and turned to face me. She started to say something, but her face scrunched up in confusion. Then she waved her thought away and pulled a loaf of bread from the refrigerator.

More country sausage sizzled in a cast iron frying pan on the stove. From a cabinet, another casserole dish hit the worktable. It wouldn't be empty long. Mom thought best in her kitchen, throwing eggs and milk together to make some magical dish. This was her Zen spot.

Mom had been silent, cubing bread and chopping bell pepper as she worked out the situation. She stopped, laying both hands flat on the worktable. "I just don't see it. I mean Wesley is the soul of civility. I never heard them even raise their voices at each other." She shook her head, another lock of hair falling to her brow. "You know, I think this is wrong. He would never hurt anybody, especially Melody."

I smiled, feeling blessed I had this woman in my life. Mom was a straight shooter who spoke the truth. And not the truth that hurt people's feelings to get a point across. She saw things through the lens of the Commandments. What was right was right, and wrong was wrong. I knew I'd have her on my side as I looked into my cousin's murder.

At that moment, I knew I had to find Melody's killer. No one else had stepped up. Besides, it was the right thing to do. Wesley would have a lawyer who could handle his legal issues. I couldn't help him. But I could make inquiries to find out who killed Melody. I was fairly sure Kelly lacked the backbone to go against the sheriff's order. I tried to understand. He had a job to protect. That didn't seem as important as finding the real killer. Tom and Anna weren't in a position to ask questions. They had a funeral to plan. Wesley was in jail.

It was up to me.

Chapter Nine

It was four in the morning, and wired from the coffee, I felt I had to do something useful. Unfortunately, the early hour made questioning people difficult. One thing I could do was secure the bakery. I was anxious to get a sign up on the door. Mom found some cardstock that could be taped or tacked to the front of the bakery. I wrote *Closed Until Further Notice*. I tucked the sign and a roll of tape in the back seat.

Securely leashed, Fido and I walked to Libby and Grant's house. The one with Grant's white Ford pickup parked in front. Lights were on in the back, in a small window, probably a bathroom. A door slammed. There were voices. The lights flashed on in the front room.

A man and a woman. Neither were happy. It sounded like a rough argument. I couldn't hear words, and my instinct was to turn and go back home. This was none of my business.

"I don't care what you say, I'm going to work." It was a young girl's voice. Obviously, it was Libby.

"I'm your father. You'll do as I say."

Fido growled.

"You're not much of a father, Grant Armstrong. I hate to even call you that."

Ouch.

"What do you mean?"

"You're never here. You don't participate in my life…"

"Be honest. Would you really like me to go to basketball games or parent-teacher night? I know you're flunking out anyway. That's one of the reasons you had to go to continuation school. It's for misfits like you." Fido's growls gave me goosebumps. It was cool outside, but the dog was obviously reacting to the heat inside the house. I turned, deciding to return home for a while to wait for the argument to subside.

"Where do you think I learned to be a jerk? From you!" Libby shouted.

"I'd say you learned from your friends, but you can't keep one. You don't know how to have a relationship." Fido held his place at the front door, still growling. I tugged at his leash, and he slowly came along.

"I'm not flunking out. That was last month. You're wrong, as always. This week alone, I got an A on my trig test. You underestimate the value of the time I spend with Melody. She's helping me with math and science. She's my one true friend. I can tell her anything. Anything."

The argument faded as I walked away. I waited ten minutes and walked back. All quiet and dark, except for the light at the back of the house. I knocked on the front door, Fido sitting obediently at my side. A hall light turned on, and I heard the doorknob turn.

A slight, young woman dressed in sweatpants and a

T-shirt answered. Purple hair cut short on one side and left long on the other was accented by a nose ring and ear tunnel jewelry. "Yes?"

"Libby? I'm Sarah Murray," I nodded toward our house. "Meg and Rob's daughter. You probably don't remember me..."

Looking past her, I saw a man in cargo-type shorts standing in the hallway, listening. Fido saw him, too, and let out a loud bark. I shushed him and focused on the man.

Grant. Medium height, dark hair, and slumped shoulders. It had been years since I'd seen him, and I couldn't have picked him out of a crowd. Thankfully, he was in his own home, so easy to identify. He turned and strode down the hall. Beside me, the dog kept up a low growl. I shushed him again, and he quieted.

"Oh, sure. I know who you are." She leaned against the jamb, still holding the door handle. A sultry grimace spread across her lips. "You're Melody's cousin, here to take over the bakery."

I sucked in a breath. This wasn't going to be easy. "That's not exactly right, Libby." I weighed the idea of explaining the arrangement but decided it would wait for another time. "I'm not here for that. I have some unwelcome news."

"What?" She gripped the doorknob, even in the poor light, her white knuckles stood out.

I hated having to tell her. But there was no getting around it, no one here to relieve me of this awful task. "Libby, Melody has been killed. Murdered."

Libby straightened and blinked furiously. For a moment, I thought she'd faint. Then slumping against the door jamb, she released a fearful groan. I grabbed her arm to steady her. "Melody? It can't be. I just saw her yesterday."

"I'm afraid it's true." I stretched out my other hand to comfort her, but, in the end, I restrained myself. Some people just didn't like being touched without permission. She seemed stable enough, so I looped the leash around my wrist and dug my hands into my jeans pockets. "For obvious reasons, the bakery won't open. We need to put a sign on the door and make sure the place is secure for now. Melody said... she gave you keys."

Fists covered her eyes as she succumbed to the shock. The girl's shoulders shook with her sobs. "No, no, no..." She repeated the denial over and over.

After a few seconds, I realized I needed to bring her back to this moment. I touched her arm. "Can I get your father here to help..."

"No." Suddenly she was wide-eyed and alert. Her eyes focused on me, and she hissed, "I don't need... anyone."

"I'm sorry for your loss, Libby." The trite words washed over her with no effect. Not that I expected them to soothe her pain. "I'm sorry to bother you after giving you this horrible news, but I need the keys to the shop, Libby. To secure it."

She exhaled a sigh that came from her toes. I brought her misery, for sure. But I wasn't going away. While I hated to intrude, there was a task that needed doing. I was sure no one else would do it. She eyed me, squinting in the gloom.

Then without a word, she disappeared into the house. Two minutes later, wrestling on a sweatshirt, she handed me a set of keys. She slammed the door behind her, dodged Fido, and stomped outside. "I'm coming with you." she snapped.

❦

The bakery was less than fifteen minutes away by car, but it was a tense ride. Libby sat in the passenger seat, sullen and sniffling, while from the back seat, Fido stared out the windshield, occasionally breathing down my neck. I asked a general question to try to break the ice but got frost in return. Let her brood. I didn't know what I could offer.

I pulled up to an alley that led to the small employee lot. Dawn was approaching, but I still needed my phone's flashlight to find the lock. The down-to-earth smell of yesterday's yeasty baked bread met me at the door as we entered the workroom. I inhaled deeply and savored the magnificence of my cousin's culinary skills. Libby followed and strode around to the largest of a pair of worktables. She put both hands on the work surface and leaned into it. A low humming noise emanated from her chest.

Fido had followed me into the room, his leash dragging on the ground. He cruised around, nose to the floor, searching for crumbs.

I left Libby at the worktable and walked out to the counter service area. Melody had planned to expand to a bakery café in the future, but for now, customers had to take their purchases home. The front was clean, simple, and elegant, with a concrete floor—same as the kitchen —with wood and glass racks and the menu posted on the wall behind the counter. Goodyear pendant lighting added an industrial influence yet made it a modern and inviting area.

Back in the work area, storage and shelves took up most of the wall space. Ovens, proofing ovens, storage racks, and stainless-steel carts each had a place. The rich aroma of spices enveloped me as I passed a shelf. This was Melody's domain. The past six months, I'd been so self-absorbed in my divorce pain and failure that I hadn't seen the shop since she opened. Now, I mourned the loss of being able to share her dream. I pictured her waltzing around worktables, mixers, shelves, past a warm oven baking a lovely tray of croissants. In my mind, she chattered on about the advantages of diverse types of flour or the overuse of sugar with her eager grin.

Libby hadn't moved from the worktable. She was silent, and enough light drifted through the windows to reveal tears on her cheeks. I stood across the table from her. Fido lay in a corner, eyes checking the room but quiet for the moment.

"You were close." I made it a statement, not a question. It was obvious.

"She saved me, you know." Libby said, finally.

Not knowing the situation, it seemed appropriate to keep a benign response. "She was a good person."

"The best." Libby's head dropped to her chest. She sighed, seemed to gather her wits, and spoke softly. "I was on a path of self-destruction. Bad choices compounded by worse ones. She saw through it before anyone else did. My dad and the school thought I was acting out because my mom died." She shrugged. "But she saw there was more to it."

From its place at the wall, she pulled a stool and sat. "She gave me a purpose. A reason to get up every morning, even if it's an ungodly hour." A hint of a smile lifted one side of her mouth. "I was even flunking out of continuation school."

"What did Melody do?"

"She gave me a job, taught me to bake, gave me a job

in this place to work on learning responsibility. She trusted me—she gave me keys, for God's sake." Libby's eyes grew intense, as if they could force me to believe her. "My Dad doesn't even know this, but I made honor roll at school this semester."

"Congratulations. Sounds like a lot of demanding work."

She nodded, staring at her hands. "It was. But she helped. While we rolled out dough, we recited the definitions of trigonometry ratios and functions." Her eyes held confusion when she looked up at me. I imagined her heart breaking. "Who does that for a neighbor kid?"

My heart melted at Melody's kindness. "Melody."

"Right." Libby studied her hands again. "I didn't make it easy for her either. But she just hung in there like a little terrier."

"That's how she was." I remembered her tenacity when she knew something was right. Once when we were in the fifth grade, my cat, Roscoe, was accused of shredding our brand-new couch. Dad was furious. He threatened to turn Roscoe outside to contend with coyotes. I was heartbroken, sure that some predator would snag my precious kitty. Melody didn't believe Roscoe had done it. She invited herself on an overnight at my house and stayed up all night to watch the sofa. Turned out, someone had left the doggie door open, and two of the barn cats came in and headed over to the couch for a shred fest. She even took pictures to prove it to my dad.

To Libby, I said, "She couldn't see you waste your life. You're worth saving. Melody would see that."

"That's just the beginning. She was much more to me..." Libby blew out an exasperated breath, her eyes focusing on me. "It's a miracle she saw anything with all her issues."

"What d'you mean, *her* issues?" Melody hadn't confided in me about any trouble. Was it the bakery? Wesley?

"Oh, that jerk from the big bakery up the street sneaking around here like a cockroach. He gave her a bad time, for sure."

My radar went up. I remember a bailiff telling me once, 'If it sounds bad, it probably is.' "What kind of 'bad time'?"

Libby stood indignant, a hand on her hip. "He started rumors that we had rats. When that was old news, he said we used expired ingredients because we were cutting corners. He tried to convince people that we were failing. Told folks not to bother lining up any loyalty to the shop because we were going under." Her voice rose to a notch below a shout.

"That's crazy. I know this place was solvent. Mel sent me a copy of her books just last month. Her counter sales increased over the past two months, and specialty orders were on the rise."

"Right?" She slapped her hand on the table. Fido raised his head, looking around at the sudden noise.

"Who is this guy? Why would he do that?"

"His name's Reginald Bateau. His mother owns the Boulangerie. The big one on Main Street." She shook her head. "As for why, you got me. He has all the money in the world. His mother practically runs the town, so it's not a power grab." Another shrug. "Who knows?"

This sounded like an interesting line of inquiry. I'd put Reginald Bateau on my list to look up.

"Oh, and one more thing," Libby said on the way to

the car. "Mel said the church organist has a crush on Wesley. I can't say that's a motive to kill Melody, but I thought you'd like to know."

I'd find Reginald Bateau right after I talk to the organist.

Chapter Ten

After making sure she'd be okay, I dropped Libby at her house and went home. Fido had a break behind the bakery before leaving and went again when he got out of the car. Mom flung open the front door, her arms laden with a box containing the casseroles. The aroma of baked jack cheese and chili casserole was heavenly. "I made two of them and prepped the French toast casserole for later. Give me a hand, will you?"

Fido thought it smelled good too. He wiggled between us. I had to pull him out of the way. He was wiggling his way into my heart too.

I yawned as I opened the passenger side door. I'd been to this dance before. I knew Mom didn't like her baked goods rolling around in the trunk. She always put everything that fit up front with her. I'd have to remember the little things like this while living under the same roof.

She slid the box onto the seat, then flashed a quizzical smile at me. She stretched a hand to my cheek.

"You look exhausted, sweetie. Why don't you take a nap?"

"I will after I see Wesley at the jail."

"Will they let you see him? I mean, it hasn't been that long since his arrest. Just a few hours, right? In my experience, the government doesn't work very fast. He might not even have been charged yet."

"Good question. I'll call Kelly." I punched the number he'd given me at the hospital.

He answered right away. "Hey, girl."

"Kelly, I've got a question for you."

"About Wesley?"

I smiled into the phone. "How'd you guess?"

"It could be that I haven't talked to you since high school graduation, and Wesley is the reason we're talking now."

"True." My cheeks grew warm. I regretted that I hadn't kept in touch with Kelly. He'd been such a nice guy in high school.

"What's your question? Maybe I can save you a trip to Independence."

Darn. Independence was the Inyo County seat where the jail was located, forty-one miles south. A tough, monotonous drive when one was tired. "Well, you answered one question. I wasn't sure if Wesley was still in Bishop or down at the county jail. Has he been charged?"

"He's been booked. He'll see a judge on Monday morning."

What day was it, anyway? I left LA on Wednesday, so today was Thursday. "Can he have visitors?"

"Mm, I'm sure. But you'll have to wait until Saturday. Visiting hours begin at nine, break for lunch..."

"Kelly. I must talk to him. I know I can't call in, but can you get a message to him to call me?"

Kelly hesitated a moment. "What's so all-fired important?"

I didn't want him to know that I was conducting my own inquiries. "I don't believe he's responsible. Did he confess?"

"Sarah, you know I can't tell you..." His voice had a slightly whiny quality to it. It was obvious that he was uncomfortable with my questions.

I needed to see him face-to-face. Begging always went easier that way, a brutal lesson learned from Blaine. "Are you still in Independence? I could meet you there. I'd like to talk to you about Wesley's mess."

"I'm at the Bishop sub." That meant the substation in the courthouse building of downtown Bishop. At least I wouldn't have to drive to Independence. "Here on over-time, writing up the report."

"Can I come see you?"

His sigh wasn't very deep. I thought he wasn't entirely resistant to seeing me. "If you can make it in the next half hour. I hope to be done and gone by then." His shift had ended hours ago, but with booking and report writing, it would be dawn before he saw his pillow. I'd heard the stories from bailiffs who transferred from the streets to the courtroom.

"I'm at my folk's place in McLaren. I'll be right over."

I put Fido in my bedroom with a bowl of water. He seemed eager to plop on the old chenille throw I'd put down for him to sleep on. I'd have to get a brush and try to get the stickers and weeds from his coat later.

Outside, I waved goodbye to my mother as we drove off in opposite directions.

The rising sun gleamed on my bug-splattered windshield as I drove into town. It took less than ten minutes for me to find the sheriff's substation door. The dayshift clerk, a short young man barely able to produce a mustache, rose to meet me at the front counter. "Deputy McSorley is with someone right now."

"Is it Sarah Murray?" Kelly's voice boomed from an office in the center of the building. When the clerk answered, Kelly yelled, "Bring her through."

The clerk buzzed open the security door and led me to an office the size of a large closet. Kelly stood beside a desk loaded with manuals, piles of paper and folders, as well as a desk organizer and PC, keyboard, and monitor. It was a wonder he got any work done. Local, state, and federal law and code books lined the wall shelves behind him. Binders with legal updates sat on a nearby table. A detailed topological map of Inyo County covered a good portion of another wall.

"Sarah." Kelly nodded. As cluttered as the room was, Kelly's frame was big enough to have filled it. But he wasn't alone. In my muddled state, as I entered, I failed to notice a tall, broad-shouldered man standing three feet to my left. Kelly held a hand up to the man. "Sarah, this is Jake Charters, Wesley's half-brother. He's a policeman from Petaluma PD up north."

Startled, I stepped back to give the man some space. He had a presence that was more than physical. "I didn't know Wesley had a half-brother." He shared Wesley's good looks, clear, penetrating brown eyes set in a pleasantly angular face topped with sandy-brown hair.

Charters directed an appraising eye over me and

returned his gaze to Kelly. "Your case isn't even circumstantial. You've got nothing."

"I was ordered to arrest him." Kelly shrugged. "Maybe the sheriff has something…"

Charters cut across Kelly's excuse. "If he did, he'd be smart to get it in the report. The DA is going to laugh you out of his office."

"Probably." I was surprised at Kelly's lack of conviction. I got the feeling he agreed with Jake Charters's conclusion.

Then, it dawned on me—Kelly didn't believe Wesley had killed Melody either. But how much help would he be to find the real killer?

Chapter Eleven

"Call me if you find my dog," Jake shouted as he swept out the door. "I bet you twenty bucks he'll find you first."

I didn't even wait to tell Kelly I'd be back. "Wait, Jake... Mr. Charters." I flew down the concrete stairs, almost bumping into him.

"What?" He stopped, his jaw set, and his eyes narrow with fury. "What do you have to add to this cluster?"

"I... I'm Melody's cousin. I'm related to Wesley by marriage." Looking into his thunderous-looking face, I lost my train of thought for a second. I must've been more tired than I thought. "But I want to tell you that I agree with you. I don't believe for a second that Wesley killed Melody."

The lines on his face relaxed, enough to take a deep breath. He nodded to a white four-wheel drive SUV. Once there, he leaned against the driver's side door. He pulled a phone from his jeans pocket. After a quick glance, he tucked it away and asked, "What makes you say that?"

Under his intense gaze, I stammered like a fourth grader. "I found Melody. In the desert, outside of Wilkerson. And I'm the one who picked up Wesley at their home." Bits and pieces of information drifted together in my brain. "Wesley had just gotten in. I know the timing is suspicious, but Wesley and Melody live on an asphalt street, not dirt. There was no dirt on his shoes. I noticed. She was assaulted in the dirt. Her shoes were dusty, his weren't."

Jake pinched his lower lip in thought. "That's not enough for an alibi, but it gives me more than gut instinct to trust him."

"I know." Relief flooded through me. I'd finally found someone who might be able to help prove Wesley innocent.

Now what? I had to ask. "Are you curious about what happened?"

His eyebrows drew together. "Of course."

I'd said it all wrong. Was there a right way to ask? I decided I had nothing to lose by cutting to the chase. "Are you going to ask around? See if there is a viable suspect walking loose out there?"

"Miss... Murray. Whatever I'm going to do, it will be alone. Alone."

If there hadn't been so much at stake, I would've been chastened, embarrassed by my prying questions. But I didn't have that luxury. "I respect that. But there are some facts you should be aware of."

"Facts?" His neck stiffened as I recognized I was pushing him away. It didn't matter. He needed to know.

"Yes. Like there's a guy in town who was pushing Melody to either fold the bakery or sell it to him. He got downright pushy."

Jake took a deep breath, opened the SUV door, and

pulled out a SF Giants ball cap. He ran his fingers through his hair, then fitted the cap on his head with the skill of a man who did this many times a day. I envisioned him in uniform tugging at his department ball cap.

"And you found this out from who?"

"Libby Armstrong, Melody's employee at the bakery."

His jaw jutted out with consideration. "Okay. What else did she say?"

I filled him in on the details, including the name of the Boulangerie owner's son.

"Interesting." His deep-brown eyes settled on me, this time with less hostility than before. In fact, with no hostility. "Anything else?"

I had a tough time not smiling with enthusiasm. I don't think I smiled. I hope I didn't smile. "Glad you asked. There's a rumor that the organist at Wesley's church was resentful of Melody. Didn't think she was good enough for him. I don't know her name." I shrugged. "I've just moved back to Bishop after being gone for a while."

"Oh yeah." he said, his eyes wandering to a place over my shoulder. I've lost his interest. He must think I'm a meddling do-gooder. He didn't care about my story.

I wondered if Jake Charters had been eliminated from the suspect list because he was a cop. I hadn't heard anything about an alibi for him. "And lastly, Sheriff Stan Dorsey is up for reelection. I've heard he's not doing well in the polls—er poll. There's only one in Inyo. He needed a boost and used Wesley's arrest to show he's on top of crime in Inyo County."

This time, Jake was listening. He nodded in agreement. "I thought McSorley was more on the ball than to make that lame arrest. That makes sense."

"Kelly is a decent guy. He tries. Dorsey didn't give him a chance to explain the case. Just gave him an order. I saw him."

"You witnessed this?"

"Yes, in the hospital lobby. Several people saw it. Dorsey humiliated Kelly in public."

Jake nodded, his lips pursed with consideration.

I had given him everything I had. There was nothing more to say, but I felt strangely reluctant to leave. "What was that you said about your dog?"

"My K-9 partner, Arco, is missing."

"Oh no." I started to get that sinking feeling. "That's awful. Have you checked the shelter?"

He slid on sunglasses and turned to get into his SUV. "I will when they open at ten."

"Wait." Oh no. It couldn't be. I had already grown attached to Fido. But this would explain his excellent training and behavior. "What breed is he?"

He stopped, one leg still on the pavement. "How did you know Arco was a male?"

"Fifty-fifty chance." I smiled, my hands open in an 'it wasn't a wild guess' gesture. "I found a male German shepherd guarding Melody's body last night. I took him home with me."

He tore his sunglasses off and squinted at me against the morning sun. "You have him?"

"Wait a minute." I backed up, feeling defensive under his scrutiny. "I said I found a German shepherd. He might not be yours."

He slid on the sunglasses again and got into the SUV. "Let's go see."

Chapter Twelve

I had no reason to say no. The idea of keeping Fido had crept into my mind and firmly anchored itself. I'd planned to return to North Sierra Vet Clinic to have his microchip scanned, and I kept my fingers crossed that we'd be unable to contact the owner. "Follow me. I'm in the white Camry."

Resigned, I went to my car and texted Kelly that I'd catch up with him later. I turned right onto West Line Street and waited for Jake Charters' white SUV to follow. Thirty seconds later, he pulled in behind me. And I don't know why I noticed, but a dark sedan drove out of the lot, following Charters.

West Line Street bisects the west side of Bishop, becomes Highway 168, and tracks all the way up to a dead end at Lake Sabrina, nineteen miles west, deep into the Sierras. From there, the terrain was too rugged to traverse to the western side of the mountains. There wasn't much vehicular traffic after the city limits, even though there were a few small housing developments and Cerro Coso Community College on the way to the lake.

I kept Charters in my rearview as I turned off to my parents' house. I pulled into our long U-shaped driveway at 1399 McLaren, making sure Charters followed. The black sedan, an older Taurus, I thought, drove on down McLaren Lane. Probably just a neighbor.

Mom's car was in the open garage. With her home, I felt better about having a stranger to the house. Charters followed close on my heels, clearly anxious to see if Fido was his.

Mom was in the kitchen putting away groceries when we walked in. "Hi, honey. Who's your guest?"

"Mom, this is Jake Charters, who may or may not own Fido."

The two shook hands. "Mr. Charters..."

"Jake, please." He gave a half smile, just like Wesley's.

"Jake, this is my mother, Meg Murray."

"It's a pleasure to meet you, Mrs. Murray."

"Call me Meg," she said, waving aside the formality. "Let's get this pup back where he belongs."

I was already down the hall. Fido hopped and whined to show he was happy to see me. He followed me into the kitchen, where Jake Charters shouted, "Arco!"

The dog whined and jumped, ecstatic to see Jake. The man knelt on one knee and rubbed the dog's head in a fierce embrace. The delight over their reunion eclipsed my dismay at having to give him up. Clearly, they were meant to be together. He stopped and inspected the bandaging on Fido's shoulder. "What happened? Did he get hit by a car?"

I shook my head. "The vet found pieces of wood in

the wound." My voice sounded tense. "He thought some-body hit him."

Jake's face hardened. "Hit him? I'd like to find the…"

"He's okay. The vet said it was a laceration and bruis-ing. If you have his health records, you might get hold of him. He said he'd hold off on the rabies shot until he knew the health history."

"I'll do that," he said, his jaw still tight with anger. "I've got to pay the vet bill anyway."

I waved that aside. The vet said he'd have the office bill me. We'd work it out later. I was busy watching the reunion. Jake's anger melted with Arco's enthusiasm to be with his human. After a minute of the master stroking the wriggling dog, Jake straightened with a smile so broad that I swear it glowed. "Yep, he's mine." Arco waited at his side.

"There wasn't any doubt." Mom said. "Can I offer you a cup of coffee?"

Jake issued a sharp command and Arco sat, alert and obedient. "That would be great."

I took a step toward Arco—he'd always be Fido to me—and asked, "Okay to pet him?" I'd heard you must ask permission to pet a service dog. I imagined it held for K-9s as well. I wasn't sure to whom it was a matter of cour-tesy, the dog or the handler.

"Sure."

I scratched under his ears, a place I'd found that he especially liked. "Mom, Jake is Wesley's half-brother."

The delight over the reunion evaporated. "Oh. I just got back from Tom and Anna's place." Mom seemed at a loss for words.

Jake rescued her. "They must be in shock." He took the coffee cup she'd offered and held it in both hands, staring at the brown liquid. "I was—am—staying with

Melody and Wes. I'd just gotten there when Arco took off. Wes was at Bible study. Melody stayed there to help me find Arco. He'd run after something, a rabbit, we think. I went one way and Mel the opposite. I was up in the hills, near an apple farm, when I saw the ambulance. I didn't make it back until everyone but the deputies had left."

"And they wouldn't tell you anything, right?" I knew enough about crime scene protocols to figure it out. This wasn't exactly an alibi. In fact, he was in the general area when Melody was assaulted. It's possible he could be determined as another suspect. Except Wesley was already in jail for Melody's murder. I wondered again if Kelly had given him a pass from the suspect list because he was a policeman. He didn't have an alibi that could be verified. Hmm.

He nodded. "I went back to the house, and the detective wouldn't let me in. That's when I figured something was really wrong. I called the hospital on a hunch. What they didn't say made me drive up there. I saw Tom. He told me Melody had died and Wesley had been arrested for her murder."

Mom cleared her throat. "I'm sure you share my daughter's belief in Wesley's innocence, Jake. But there's something you should know."

Jake put down the coffee mug and reached for Arco's head in an automatic gesture. I braced myself for unwelcome news.

"Anna attends Wesley's Bible study every Wednesday." Mom shook her head, her light-brown hair brushing her shoulders. She didn't like having to tell us this. "Thing is, Anna said Wesley canceled the class last night."

Chapter Thirteen

I stood on the driveway with one hip leaning on Jake's SUV, the morning sun warming my face. Arco sat waiting in the back seat. Jake seemed reluctant to leave, so I ventured a guess. "It's just a matter of time before the sheriff's detective gets that information. Dorsey didn't care about Wesley's alibi before, and now any possibility has vanished."

He nodded, deep in thought. "Where was Wes?"

"I have no idea. Kelly's sent a message to have Wesley call me. I can ask then. Time is critical since his arraignment will be early next week. I won't be able to see him in person until Saturday during the jail's visiting hours."

"Wait, wait, wait." Jake held his hand up like he was directing traffic. "You can't go snooping around."

Did he worry that I'd find out something about him? "Oh really? Why?" He was telling me what I could and couldn't do. A perfect stranger... and one who didn't have an alibi either.

"This is a murder case. You're not a cop, and you are too close to the suspect."

"What you say is true." My hands went to my hips. No way he was dictating to me. "But being a civilian has its benefits. I'm not bound by the same rules you are. Besides, you're an outsider here. You can't ask these locals questions."

"What makes you think I'm going to ask anyone anything?" His voice got a little louder. I was glad we were outside, away from my mother. I wouldn't want her to see us arguing.

I looked him straight in the eye. "First, because you know him and don't believe Wesley killed Melody any more than I do." I counted off the reasons on my fingers. "Second, you're related. And third, this arrest is all wrong. Too many questions aren't even being asked."

He smiled and then ran his fingers through his hair. "You're something, Sarah…"

"And fourth, *you* are too close, but it doesn't make a difference to you."

He'd had enough. "Okay, okay." He held his hands before him in a 'give up' gesture. "I bet you've got a suggestion for the next move."

Maybe he was relenting, letting me in. He knew more about investigating than I did. "We need to find out why Wesley canceled the Bible study and where he was. We can do that over the phone if he calls me. Until then, I'd like to talk to the organist from the church."

Jake considered this.

I felt like I still needed to convince him. "It may be a mere rumor, but I want to see what she says. People have murdered for less." Jake eyed me skeptically. "I'm a former court reporter from Los Angeles County, so I know the trial case legalities. It's the investigation that I need help with."

"All right. You're in. Any idea when Wes will call you?"

"Not a clue. But I'm keeping my phone with me."

"Okay. What about the organist? Who is she, and how do we get hold of her?"

I thought a moment. "I'll see if Mom or Anna know what her name is. But I warn you, Bishop people are friendly to a degree. This is a difficult situation, and it's likely they're not going to speak to a stranger about one of their own. Here's where I can be of help."

Jake nodded, accepting the plan. He waited while I went back in the house. Mom knew the organist's name and where she worked, but that was all. Back outside, I googled the business, called, and found out she was a driver for the county transit system. She was currently out of the immediate area, but she got off work at five o'clock. I gave Jake the address of the county yard and arranged to meet him there at five.

Fatigue finally caught up with me. I felt like I could drop right there. "I need to take a quick nap. I've been up all night. You look like you could use some sleep too."

"Now I have Arco, I think I can take a nap." Jake chuckled. "And we have a plan." He gave a thumbs-up sign and climbed into his SUV.

We said our goodbyes, and he drove off, Arco barking happily in the back of the SUV. In my room, I ruefully noticed the faint smell of dog. I missed Arco already, after only having him for a few hours. After a glance around, I decided to unpack later. I could use a shower, but instead, I fell into bed with all my clothes on and my phone beside my pillow.

Chapter Fourteen

My phone alarm went off at 4:30 p.m. Deeply asleep, it took me a minute to orient myself. Oh yeah. My parents' house, my old bedroom, made over to accommodate guests. Blaine and I slept here when we came for visits. It had felt slightly sacrilegious then, and downright revolting now. I hated to think about where he'd been and who he'd been with.

My hair was still wet from the shower when I pulled up on the road shoulder in front of the county bus yard. Less than a mile from the house on West Line Street, I was able to make time for that shower.

In addition to county maintenance equipment and vehicles, transit buses were serviced and stored here. A chain-link fenced parking lot to the south of the compound held what looked like parked employee cars.

Jake arrived minutes later with Arco in the back seat, barking at me. Jake got out and whistled to Arco, who bounded out of the SUV and up to me. I bent to scratch his ears and laughed when he licked my face. After a minute, Jake called Arco back to the vehicle and adjusted the windows to allow ventilation.

Mom had given me a basic description of Vernelle Kearney—medium height, curly blond hair usually in a ponytail, and mousy with rimless glasses. Jake and I waited, eyeing the half dozen employees leaving at the end of their day shift. Transit buses rumbled past us, spewing exhaust as they accelerated out the driveway.

Jake spotted her, pointing silently. Together, we walked across the asphalt lot and intercepted her as she got to her dented Ford Escort.

"Vernelle Kearney?" I spoke, as Jake and I had agreed. He'd add questions as needed, but I took the lead on this.

Vernelle whipped around to face me, her eyes red and chin trembling. "What?"

"Vernelle, I'm Sarah Murray. I'm related to Wesley, and I'd like to talk to you about his innocence."

"What?" She sniffled, wiping her nose on the cuff of her sleeve. "Related?"

I wondered how competent she was to drive Highway 395 all day. She didn't seem aware of her surroundings but seemed consumed with grief. I had to get her talking.

"Yes, we're cousins." I fudged the truth here, but she needn't know I was related to Wesley by marriage to my cousin. "He always spoke so highly of you, Vernelle." Now I was surely going to hell for lying.

She squinted, trying to understand what I said. "Really? I didn't think he knew I was alive."

"He did. He said you were an honest, trustworthy person." I was going to hell for sure.

Vernelle's shoulders straightened. "Really?"

"Yes. So, I was wondering…"

"Yes?" I had her attention, what there was of it.

"Do you know why Wesley canceled his Bible study class last night?"

"No." She sniffed into a battered tissue. "He didn't say in his email. Just that something important had come up that had to be attended to."

"Do you have any ideas where he went? What he was doing?"

Vernelle's head turned both ways. We were the only people around. The other drivers had already left. "I can only guess."

I felt Jake tense beside me. He was getting impatient with Vernelle's reticence. So was I.

"I'll listen to your guess, Vernelle."

She stepped closer to me, ignoring the silent Jake. "I think he was following his wife."

This caught me by surprise. I wasn't ready for this line of inquiry. But I had to ask. "Because…"

"I think he believed Melody was cheating on him." She straightened, pleased with her accusation. "She probably was, you know." She searched my expression to see if I believed her. I struggled to keep it blank in the face of her suppositions. "She always thought she was better than everyone else. Snooty. That's the word. She was snooty. Certainly not good enough for Wesley."

"Yes, I'm sure you're right." It cut to my heart to say that, to agree with unfounded rumors. At least, I hoped they were unfounded. "I'm sorry Wesley canceled the Bible study. I hope it didn't inconvenience you."

She shrugged. "Not really. I read the email at work, so I grabbed a Burger King, ate dinner at home, and watched *The Real Housewives of New Jersey*."

"Too bad you had to stay in all by yourself." I sympathized with her.

She shrugged again, not knowing her alibi had taken wing. "Did you ever see Melody with anyone?"

"Anyone? She was the minister's wife. She had people around her all the time. If you're asking if I ever saw her with someone special, I can tell you that she spent a lot of time at church talking to the police chief's son. Young man, good-looking, short attention span. You know the type." For the first time, she acknowledged Jake standing nearby. He'd been quiet, watching. Vernelle poked an elbow at me and nodded at Jake. "Not like this guy. He listens. A good trait in a man. You got a good one there, lady."

My face flushed, a dozen protests coming to mind. I glanced at Jake, and his face was impassive, unreadable. In the end, I said nothing, not wanting to jeopardize any further information I might get.

Vernelle flipped her wrist and scowled. "Oh, look at the time. I gotta pick up my aunt for bingo."

We said our goodbyes and, from the front seat of Jake's SUV, watched her drive off. Fido—Arco—huffed and whined behind us, signaling a break was in order.

"I've gotta take Arco out, but I don't want to do it here. It's too close to the road. How about a walk on Mumy Road?

He drove the SUV another mile west on West Line Street. We took a left on Mumy Road, a rural ribbon of asphalt laid across cattle pastures lined with straggly cottonwood trees. With no homes or businesses, Mumy was a neglected road often used by walkers and runners. We parked on the shoulder near West Line Street.

Arco bounded out of the SUV and promptly began his business. Jake and I strolled behind him, tossing a stick every now and then. The sun in the western sky would soon drop behind the Sierras. Dusk here stretched on longer than it had in Los Angeles. For the first time since I arrived, I took the time to savor the day. It felt good to be home.

"What do you think about Vernelle?" Jake interrupted my thoughts.

"She's got a crush on Wesley and is, er, was jealous of Melody, for sure." I shrugged. "As for being a killer," I hesitated, then shook my head. "I don't think she's got the nerve."

"Ah, but that's if you're speaking to premeditation." Jake tossed a stick, and Arco ran after it, his tongue hanging outside his mouth. "An accident is more likely."

"You're right. Behavior-wise, I didn't see any remorse or necessary justification in her."

"We'll just keep her on our suspect list. She might be a good actress."

"Maybe."

"There's something I want to tell you." He stopped and looked out over the valley. I had the feeling that whatever he was going to tell me wasn't pleasant. "I feel like I need to be honest with you."

I stopped. This sounded like high school theatrics. My opinion of him dropped a notch even before he spoke. Darn it, I was just growing to like him. "Go on." My voice sounded defiant.

"I'm feeling like we're starting a good friendship here…"

At his pause, I encouraged his next thought. "Yes…"

"It feels less than honest if I don't tell you now."

Tell me what? That you're a serial killer? You collect stamps? That you skipped kindergarten? My mind raced, considering and rejecting the possibilities. But I hadn't considered this one.

"I lost my wife to cancer four years ago." He raised his hand at my reaction. "Wait. I'm not asking for sympathy. I just want you to know because this is a small town. I didn't want you to hear it from anyone else."

"I'm so sorry." What a fool I could be.

He shrugged. "I know. Me too. But there was nothing to be done. We tried all the treatments, chemo and radiation, surgery, and finally, the doctors said to take her home so she could have some peace."

"You know what Wesley is going through."

"The grief part, yes." He picked up a stick and threw it. Arco charged after it. "But no one ever arrested me for killing Kristin."

I shook my head at the absurdity. "That complicates things."

"It does. Now he's not only dealing with his grief but has to worry about defending himself."

"It's good of you to be here for him."

"I'm reciprocating what he's done for me."

"He stayed with you?"

He bent to pick up the spit-covered, gnawed stick. He threw it once again. "Mel too. She came up with him and took over for a week. They both organized the funeral and reception afterward. Even knowing that was the end, I was still in shock. I couldn't function. Wes got help from the department, and between them both, I crawled through it. Dad was there too. I shouldn't shortchange his efforts. He's just not always the most positive person to have around in a situation like this. Wes came up for a few days every month to make sure I was on the right track. And, I have to say, he is a significant reason I'm in one piece today. I owe these two people my life."

"Thank you for sharing this with me." We stopped at

his SUV. "I'm so sorry about your wife. I can't imagine that kind of loss."

He stood at the back hatch while Arco jumped in. Jake leaned on the door post and rubbed his eyes. "I wouldn't wish it on my worst enemy."

I put my hand on his arm and gave him what I hoped was a compassionate smile. "And now you're here to help your brother."

He flashed a wry smile. "I'm glad you dropped the 'half' in front of brother. I will too."

"People will wonder where you were while Wesley was going to grammar and high school here." This was a small town, after all. People had long memories.

"Let them wonder."

He was right. Bishop was like a huge family. Some people you knew plenty about, some not so much. No one needed all the details of another's life. "How good is the attorney your father hired?"

"Dad's not rich, but he wouldn't skimp on a matter this grave. I don't know the attorney's name or reputation, but he says he'll get Wes released right away. That counts in his favor as ambitious. If Dad didn't have heart problems, he'd be here now. He can't take the altitude."

"Does he live up there in the North Bay with you?"

"Not with me, but yes, he lives in Marin County, about twenty minutes south of Petaluma."

"Nice to have him so close." My phone vibrated in my jeans pocket.

I pulled it out and groaned inwardly. It was Blaine. I couldn't think of any reason to answer it. Maybe something was wrong with Rusty. That would be the only reason I'd want to hear from my ex-husband. The phone kept ringing while I debated. When the call went over to voicemail, I turned it off and shoved it in my pocket.

Jake was silent, but when I glanced at him, he had a raised eyebrow. The phone chime indicated the voicemail was complete. Before I could put the phone back in my pocket, it rang again.

"Maybe it's..." The screen said Inyo County Jail. "It's Wesley."

Chapter Fifteen

"Sarah, it's so good to hear your voice." Wesley sounded hoarse and tired.

"You, too, Wesley." Where to start? Did you kill your wife? Was she having an affair? These questions were too brutal on top of what he was already suffering. Besides, the calls are recorded. I didn't want to compromise his defense before he even had one organized.

"My father's arranged for an attorney. He got one from LA, I think. Dad doesn't trust these Podunk lawyers around here. We'll see if he can get me out." He sighed. "Did you meet my brother?"

"Yes. He's with me now. You want to speak to him?"

"In a minute. I just want to know something. Sarah, do you believe me? I couldn't kill Melody. She's the love of my life."

"Yes, Wesley. I know you didn't kill her. But there is one thing that bothers me." I waited for him to tell me to go on. He didn't. But I did anyway. "Why did you cancel the Bible study last night? Where did you go?"

"You know these lines are recorded, right? We'll talk another time."

I had to resign myself to trust him for now. "Here's your brother."

"Yo." Jake said into my phone. They spoke for a few minutes, mostly about their father and attorneys. There were a pair of cats at Wesley's home that needed to be fed. Jake assured him that he kept Arco away from them. Then Jake handed me the phone.

"Sarah, thanks for taking care of the bakery. I assume you've closed it. The church office would be shut for now. The secretary, Mrs. Mello, would've handled it."

"I'm doing what I can, Wesley." I hated to broach the subject and wasn't at all sure he would answer. "We spoke to Vernelle Kearney today. I got the feeling she was jealous of Melody. I think she has a crush on you, Wes."

He sighed. "She's been acting really familiar since she came to my church last year, so I guess it's not totally unexpected." He paused. "And no, it's not reciprocated." I could almost see him shudder over the phone.

"Okay. I want to ask one more question. I've heard that Melody showed special interest in the police chief's son. Is that correct?"

"Where'd you hear that tripe from?" Wesley snapped. "Oh, of course. Vernelle. No, it's not true. That kid's got problems but there's nothing romantic between him and Mel. My wife's a really good listener and she's helping the boy sort out his issues."

I thought it sad that Wesley spoke of his wife in the present tense. Denial? Grief? Shock?

I figured I could get the name of the boy from another source, so I told him I'd see him on Saturday during jail visiting hours.

Chapter Sixteen

After disconnecting, I felt less optimistic than I had before. He hadn't told me anything new. Plus, his noncommittal answers left too much room for suspicion.

"You okay?"

"Yes." I answered automatically. I didn't know Jake well enough to share my doubts with him. Besides, I wasn't convinced he didn't know more about this than he was telling. Because he was in the area of Melody's assault, I had trouble believing that he hadn't seen or heard anything. Sound travels easily over the desert. There are no obstructions.

We'd walked almost a mile. "It's time we get back."

Jake bent to grab Arco's stick, a piece of desiccated cottonwood from a fallen branch. Tooth marks punctuated the wood and reminded me how strong this dog's jaw was. Jake turned to follow me, whistling for Arco. The dog ran past us, anticipating the stick being thrown in the new direction.

Jake hesitated, stick in hand, while Arco whined with anticipation. I followed Jake's gaze to West Line

Street, wondering what made him react so dramatically. I could just see the roadway. There it was—a dark sedan. The one that had followed me home to McLaren.

"That car... it followed us from the substation to my house." I stared at him. "You saw it too?"

"It was behind my car, so yeah. I saw it. This makes it twice in one day. What're the odds of the same dark sedan following us twice in one day?"

"In Bishop? It's possible, but..."

"Thought so." His jaw tensed, an action that was becoming familiar. "Look normal so we can get closer." Jake tossed the stick, trying to act normal. I watched him out of the corner of my eye.

We walked, picking up our pace gradually as we approached West Line Street. Two hundred feet away, the car started. Gravel flew up in a dusty cloud from accelerating tires. Headed eastbound toward town, all I saw was a male driver.

Jake frowned. "I didn't expect to get close, but at least this tells us one thing."

"What does it tell us?"

"Someone's following either you or me. I haven't spent much time over here, so no one besides Melody's family really knows me. It must be you." His brown eyes focused on me. But something was working very hard behind them.

"That doesn't make sense." I dismissed the idea with the wave of a hand. "Why would anyone want to keep tabs on me?"

Jake gave a sharp command, and the stick dropped from Arco's mouth. He picked it up and tossed it again. I got the feeling he was thinking his ideas through. "Consider this—your cousin's husband was arrested for her murder. But you're asking questions, talking to strangers."

I took a deep breath and paused, staring at the trickling creek beside the lane. "Someone doesn't want you casting any doubt on Wes' guilt."

"Questions lead to answers, and you think the answers could give Wesley an alibi? Or even prove him innocent?" The idea took root. As much as I didn't want to believe any of my neighbors could be responsible for Melody's death, I believed someone other than Wesley killed her. Is that person trying to cover up his tracks? "Do you think whoever did this is trying to intimidate me into backing off?"

He shrugged, staring a long way off at the Eastern Sierra mountains, maybe thinking about the insurmountable problems he was bringing up. There was no road across this chunk of the mountain range. The nearest highway over to the western side was ninety minutes north to Tioga Pass through Yosemite Park. To the south, it was a two-and-a-half-hour drive south to Highway 14 to Bakersfield. We faced similar barriers. Finally, he ignored his reluctance and said, "Maybe the sheriff has this crime all tied up in a neat little package and doesn't want you pulling the strings loose."

I rubbed my eyes at the enormity of what had been proposed, the dread settling into my bones. "Even if either point is true, it won't stop me."

Jake was silent, Arco at his side panting.

"It's not right." I faced him, my hand on his forearm. "Whoever is behind this or whatever the reason, the killer must be discovered. I won't let Wesley be punished for something he didn't have a hand in."

The water flowed past us; the snow melt was on its way to irrigate hay fields in Coso Junction near Pearsonville. He said, "You understand this could jeopardize your job prospects."

"I'm not stopping." I took a deep breath, envisioning myself living with my parents forever. "I won't ask for your help. You have a job to consider too."

"You wouldn't want to feel responsible if I lost my job too, right?" A smile touched one side of his mouth. "Wesley's my brother. Granted, we didn't spend much time together growing up—different mothers made it awkward. But we've grown close in the past few years."

It was my turn to listen.

"What he—and Mel—did for me a few years ago, I'll never forget. I owe them. Both."

I kept my mouth shut in case he wanted to talk.

He didn't, at least not about his past. "If you can't depend on your brother, the cop, to get you out of trouble, what good is he?" He turned to face me, his hand extended. "We'll find the real killer together."

When we shook, the warmth and strength of his hand surprised me. It triggered something I hadn't felt in years. "Deal."

Chapter Seventeen

J ake and I planned to meet at the Boulangerie tomorrow morning. The short nap I'd taken this afternoon was wearing thin, so I headed home. I drove down the narrow McLaren Road, noticing the neighbors' house lights on. The dusk had deepened, and I hadn't noticed the lateness of the hour. I parked my Camry off the driveway on the gravel. I loved this car. It had been a constant, unfailing friend to me since things began to turn ugly at home. The Camry had been my escape from the arguments and disappointments and, ultimately, from the divorce. Knowing I would be relocating to Bishop, I trusted this car would make the drive. I didn't anticipate going to LA again anytime soon, but the idea of a vehicle breakdown in the desert was not one I relished. Still, my adventure on Wilkerson roads left me thinking about a four-wheel drive vehicle.

I sat in the driver's seat, reviewing the events of the day, in particular, the dark sedan. I shivered as I thought about what it could mean. Someone was tracking my movements and watching me. Not for the first time, I wished I had Arco beside me.

A light shone from Libby's house. Grant's car wasn't in the open garage, but there was another—a sedan. I'd never noticed it before. This morning Libby said she hadn't wanted to confide in her father. I needed to check on her. I got out and locked my car. Old habits from the big city are hard to break, even in Bishop.

Libby answered at the first knock. She seemed breathless, and I wondered what I was interrupting. She welcomed me inside and pointed to the kitchen table. "I just made a kettle of hot water for tea. You want a cup?"

I dropped into a chair and took in the kitchen while she poured the tea water. It was a single-story ranch-style home, a similar floor plan and vintage as my parents' but with no improvements. Cracked and chipped tile countertops capped white pine cabinets. It had been years since the walls had seen a coat of paint or a bottle of 409. A portable dishwasher sat cocked sideways in a corner while the dish drainer next to the sink overflowed with drying dishes. Decades-old, framed pictures of coffee pots and artsy vegetables hung on one wall. Another had two shelves with dusty cookbooks resting on them. This is what the room must have looked like when Libby's mother passed away.

At least the dishes in the drainer looked clean. I didn't inspect them.

"Thanks, Libby. This is just the pick-me-up I need." At home, Mom would've put a dinner plate with left-overs in the microwave as she used to. Suddenly I felt very hungry. "I just wanted to check on you. I know you and Melody were close, and this is such a shock—to everyone."

"It's even worse that Wesley got arrested." Libby put

her tea mug down with a clatter. "I just don't see it. They were, like, the happiest couple I knew."

I nodded. Visions of their small wedding filled my head. Melody on Tom's arm, walking down the aisle, Tom beaming so broadly I thought his face would break. Their vows, so serious, yet with a humorous line about the wife "obeying" her husband. I was in LA when she had a miscarriage and drove up that day to be with her. I found my presence consoled her but wasn't necessary. Wesley stayed by her side for days afterward, a constant source of solace and support.

"I know." I wished Blaine had a quarter of Wesley's commitment to their marriage. I pushed the thought away. I was here for Libby. I looked across the table at this lost soul who had been found, and now, might be lost again. "Tell me more about how Melody saved you."

Libby drew in a deep breath. "She gave me a job and the trust that I'd do it right. I already told you about school. She was grooming me to take over the business when she got too old to run it. I would've too. My AA is in hospitality management. And..." Libby stopped with a coy look. "She really knew about people. I mean, relationships."

"She helped you with a relationship?"

"Not me. Someone I care about."

"Was this recent?" I don't know why I asked. I was looking for breadcrumbs that might lead me to a murderer. The police chief's son? That seemed a stretch, but one worth following up.

Libby nodded. "The past two weeks. Even though she was so torn up about Reggie-baby's threats, she made time for my friend." Reggie-baby had to be Reginald Bateau. Jake and I would see him tomorrow. We'd try to nail down the origin of the 'threats' and rumors against Layers.

"Libby, can you tell me the name of your friend?"

She straightened; any confidence had flown out the window.

I rushed to make my point. "It could be important, Libby. We need to know everything about where she was, what she was doing, who she was talking to. Someone other than Wesley killed her. The sheriff has closed this case so a murderer will go free, and an innocent man will go to prison. Please, Libby. Help me find the killer."

Her fingers twisted a lock of her purple hair. "I can't. I promised."

"Can you reach this person and have them call me?"

She brightened. A solution to her dilemma. "I can do that."

I pulled out my cell and texted her my phone number. I was sure I wouldn't know the name of the person who would call—maybe.

Chapter Eighteen

Eight-thirty felt too early for anything, much less coffee and croissants. I had a feeling the sleep I'd lost yesterday would never be made up. Even after a lovely, long bubble bath, I had trouble finding sleep. My mind raked through all the information that Jake and I had collected. In the end, I had to conclude that I didn't know much more than yesterday morning. I must've slept soundly when sleep came because I almost fell out of bed at the alarm.

I showered, managed a little mascara to dress up my jeans and cotton blouse, and met Jake inside the Boulangerie. Two cups of coffee steamed on the table as Jake waved me over.

His smile told me he was happy to see me. "I knew you'd be on time."

There it was—Sensible Sarah. Well, I was getting tired of it. Making responsible choices and doing what everyone expects is boring. I'd married the guy my parents approved of, I'd moved to Los Angeles to start married life with him and a career in the high-powered

LA legal landscape. A little voice whispered, "How's that working out for ya?"

I snorted in an undignified manner and answered. "Bad habit."

"Ouch, bad mood?"

"No," I snapped, testifying to his truth. "I'm just tired of being sensible and predictable."

Jake sat back, a smile creeping onto his lips. "So far, I've seen very little evidence of you being predictable." He took a sip of the hot coffee. "The jury's out on sensible."

I frowned and noticed a table of young women sitting kitty-corner watching him and whispering. Touristy types, rock climbers. They all wore ponytails, sunblock shirts, and ripstop pants.

"Did you find out if Reggie-baby is here?" I sipped my coffee, burning my tongue.

"Reggie-baby?"

"That's what Libby calls him. I stopped by and talked with her last night. She says Melody was," my fingers wiggled in air quotes "—counseling—a friend of hers. She's going to have him call me."

"Ah. Reggie-baby will join us for coffee and croissants in a few minutes. Any idea how you want to play this? If we do good cop, bad cop, you should be the bad cop. You're already halfway there." He chuckled at his own joke.

I slapped my cup down, splashing hot coffee on my fingers. "Ow. Get me a napkin. *Please*." I guess I had that coming. I needed to chill.

I inspected my fingers as a pudgy, red-haired man with a hawk-like nose approached the table with a tray of two croissants. He slid the tray on the table and pulled up a chair. "Here you go." He glanced from Jake to me and said, "I'm Reginald Bateau. What did you want to see me about again? The clerk wasn't clear."

After introductions, he peered at me. "You're Rob Murray's daughter, aren't you?" At my nod, he continued. "Rob and I were on the McLaren Water Board a few years ago. Now, what can I do for you?"

I took a deep breath and began. "I'm sure you heard about Melody Charters' murder."

He managed a mournful look. "Yes, and a horrible thing it is."

I sat back in my seat and gave him my best glare. "Really? I heard you couldn't wait to put her out of business." Even watching Reginald, I saw Jake's eyes widen. I didn't want to tiptoe around him and any excuses he might raise.

"Don't be silly..."

"Reginald, you spouted rumors about her business failing, unsanitary practices, and about cockroaches in her kitchen." I tsked. "Honestly, if her husband wasn't already in jail for it, the sheriff would do well to look at you. I heard you even offered to buy her out."

"Lady, you're off your rocker." He stood, upending his chair. "You don't dare come into my place of business and accuse me of a heinous murder. Get out."

We were done here. Bad mood or not, I'd gotten the gist of his temperament. I'm not sure I wouldn't have reacted the same way in the face of the accusations I'd thrown at him. But I'd seen what I wanted. He had a temper.

Reginald Bateau was certainly on my suspect list.

Chapter Nineteen

Standing in the Boulangerie parking lot at my car, I glanced around. The Owens Valley was glowing with the promise of summer. Improbable green plant life flourished in the middle of the desert. Mountain peaks of the Sierras and Nevada's White Mountains were still capped in snowy white, but at lower elevations, the weather was milder. A breeze rustled the surrounding cottonwood trees. Sometimes spring breezes are more like windstorms, but today was mild. I didn't even need a sweater. Across the street, City Park was a jewel set in the valley. I heard little kids squealing with play. Ducks quacked in the lovely duck pond set in the middle.

A deep sadness descended on me. Melody would never see this. We would never enjoy her ebullient laugh or infectious enthusiasm. I didn't know what part Reginald Bateau had in this mess, but his motive was obvious for getting rid of Melody and her business.

One ugly job done, and I needed to face another. It was time for me to visit Tom and Anna. Giving them my condolences was a necessary part of life in a small town.

Being related to practically half the town also made it a familial duty. I hated that I must do this.

Jake stood by patiently, waiting for me. When I looked at him, he smiled. "You were a million miles away."

"I was." I collected myself. "But now I have to go to Tom and Anna's to make a consolation visit. I'm dreading it."

He nodded with understanding. "How about we meet up this afternoon to compare notes and decide where to go from here?"

"That sounds fine. Call or text when you're ready."

We headed off in different directions. I stopped off at my parents' house for a casserole dish I'd put together this morning and headed over.

Chinese Hash

- *1 lb. ground beef*
- *1 stalk celery*
- *1 medium onion*
- *1 clove garlic*
- *3-4 mushrooms (optional)*
- *½ bell pepper*
- *1 can Cream of Chicken soup*
- *1 can Cream of Celery or Mushroom soup*
- *2 cups white or brown rice-cooked*
- *½ c (2 tbs.) soy sauce*
- *½ tsp. pepper*
- *1 8-oz can of water chestnuts, diced*
- *3 oz. Chinese Chow Mein noodles*

Cook rice in 2 cups of water for 15 mins. Brown beef. Sauté diced onions, celery, and pepper. Add mushrooms and water chestnuts late. Stir soup, soy sauce, and pepper into the browned beef. Mix rice and beef in a large bowl. Pour into a large casse-role. Cover and bake at 350 degrees for 20-30 minutes. Uncover. Sprinkle with noodles. Return to oven and bake an additional 5 minutes.

Serves 4

Dad's truck was parked in the driveway, and I pulled in behind him. My dashboard screen lit up, indicating a phone call from Blaine. I pushed the silence button on my phone and got out.

Anna, eyes red-rimmed and puffy, opened the door without her customary welcome. I slipped the casserole into her hands. Her movement was automatic, no thought given to the contribution when my mother appeared at her elbow and took it from her. That was the purpose of the casserole—so Anna wouldn't have to cook to feed the many people surrounding them for solace. Mom disappeared into the kitchen to allow for a quiet moment between aunt and niece. When Anna met my gaze, she gasped with the sob in her chest and reached out for a bear hug. "I just saw her. She was here for a recipe, then went home and…" She didn't let go for a long time. I held her in my embrace, caressing her shoulder as if it could wipe away her grief. As the mother of my best friend, Anna had become my second mother. I knew the depth of love she had for her daughter.

When Anna finally recovered, she showed me in. Tom and Dad sat at the kitchen table. Each gripped a mug of coffee, hanging on as if there was the possibility the coffee could make sense of this tragedy. Mom fussed about the counter, making a sandwich for me, while

Anna hovered near the refrigerator, her swollen eyes vacant with loss. This wasn't the first child she'd lost.

A pair of young cousins from Yerington, Nevada, on Tom and Mom's side, had arrived after me and, after hugs and tears, bustled in the back of the house, setting up for more visitors. In the abyss of grief was the consolation of family love, each one doing their best to lighten the Gibsons' burden. Had Anna not been in shock, she'd have been in the middle of the organizing.

I sat beside Dad, a tall, wiry outdoors-type seen often in the valley. Dad was in his early sixties and made his living as an optometrist. Dad was more the L.L. Bean guy to Tom's cowboy, but he'd hardly left Tom's side since hearing the news. Sitting so close by, I felt his frustration and impotence at not being able to help his family in their anguish. I sat down with them. We chatted about mindless, inconsequential things, trying to impose a state of normalcy. But after a few minutes, talk would stop, and sighing into coffee mugs resumed.

Finally, Tom's tired eyes scanned the table—Dad, Mom, and I, with Anna hovering around the stove. "I just don't understand. Why Melody? And the thought of Wesley... being responsible defies reason."

Anna glanced over her shoulder. "Sarah, you're the sensible one. What do you think?"

All the eyes in the room zoomed to me. Consideration for Tom and Anna's feelings was utmost in my mind, but I had to be honest. Looking Tom in the eye, I said, "I agree that Wesley isn't who I would've arrested. At this point, I don't know who else could be held accountable." I took a deep breath. "As for the explanation? None of us mere mortals can answer that, Uncle Tommy."

I know my words had little effect on them. I was still

reeling myself. What could take away the shock and the pain of losing Melody? Only time and faith in God that better days are ahead.

The lines on Tom's face deepened as he shut his eyes against the tears. "Why?"

I left a few minutes later, feeling more than inadequate. A failure, I thought. As though man in his hubris can explain a sudden, violent death like this. Like an explanation will extinguish the pain and anguish of loss. There were no words. No answers.

I sat in my car, my head on the headrest, thinking about the past hour. With the realization that no one could take on their misery, I knew I could do *something*. Like finding the person responsible. Yes, I'd committed to discovering who had killed my cousin. But today, I witnessed the cruelty visited on the family of a murdered person. I knew exposing the killer wouldn't remove the family's pain, but it might ease it. I vowed to double down and make this my mission to find the person who killed Melody and free Wesley.

I did gain one new piece of information—Anna said Melody left to go home at 7:00 p.m. I wasn't sure how that fit into the time frame, but another piece of the puzzle slipped together.

With renewed conviction, I pushed the ignition button of my car. A voicemail notification chimed on my phone. I sighed. Blaine. Against my best instincts, I pushed the playback button.

"Hey Sarah, it's me. I want you to know that our mutual dog is having some difficulty with you being gone. I'll be taking him to the vet, but I thought you should know. Call me if you want news. He misses you. I miss you."

Difficulty? Rusty was ill? He'd always been so hardy.

Possibilities churned in my mind—ulcer, behavior problems? And I'd understood dogs could be depressed—what about that?

What about a ploy? A way to get me to call him.

Well, it was going to work. I decided to call him back because I care about Rusty.

I braced myself and dialed.

Chapter Twenty

The phone rang while I checked the clock. He'd called a little over an hour ago from the landline that had been at our house. I was surprised the phone service was still on. Escrow would close tomorrow, so I expected he'd be there with cleaners or painters. Whatever. The ringing stopped, and after a click, Blaine's rushed voice answered. "Sarah? Sarah?" His voice was harsh, and my mind immediately went to Rusty. "Is Rusty okay? What happened?"

"Sarah, it's good to hear your voice."

Impatient for news, I cut across his greeting. "What's going on with Rusty?"

"Um, Rusty's as well as can be expected..."

"As well as can be... is he sick or something?" My heart thumped wildly in my chest. I should've taken Rusty. Blaine had no business keeping that dog. He was a movie location scout for crying out loud. He researched, visited, and photographed different, often international, locations for movies and commercials. That meant frequent travel, long workdays, and an unpredictable schedule. It was his occupation that had enabled his philandering while we were married. How could I tell what was work and what wasn't? It also meant Rusty would have to be boarded or dog sat for days on end. Why did I let him talk me into keeping Rusty?

"No, Sarah. It's okay." I pictured him with both hands up, trying to stop my rushing concern. He'd used that gesture often in the past year. "Rusty's just depressed. He wasn't eating, so I took him to Dr. Anders. He's lost five pounds, you know. The vet thinks it's because you left without him." The hook was baited and set.

I took it anyway and ran with it. "I'll offer again to take him. He'll have stability and a regular routine here."

"Well, I'm thinking about that."

I started with surprise. Letting me have Rusty?

"Really?" When did I sound so pathetic?

"What I was thinking was, why don't you come home, and we can..."

My spine went steely. "Blaine. *We* don't have a home, remember? You called from there, I know, but it closes tomorrow. It's a done deal. There is no *we* anymore."

"Baby," I hated when he called me that. It sounded so *Hollywood*. "This isn't the only house in Southern California. We can..."

"We can't, Blaine. We are over. It's done. The divorce is final in the eyes of the court and mine."

He was silent, regrouping for the next onslaught. I found it unbelievable that he wanted to be together after all these months of turmoil. I'd heard that he'd had a lady friend and figured he wanted his freedom and new girlfriend more than me. A thought occurred to me.

"Blaine, did your new girlfriend dump you?"

He sputtered an answer that wasn't entirely clear.

"She did, didn't she? That's what this is about." He'd

needed my income while we were married to get us through the lean times when movies weren't paying much for scouts or between jobs. He never could save a dime. Anything we had was because I took over our finances the last year, leaving his salary to him. Maybe his new girlfriend caught on quicker than I had. I shook my head with disbelief. "Some things never change, Blaine. Neither do you. Unless you want to give me Rusty, this conversation is over."

Sensible Sarah. Finally sensible in my own life. I pushed disconnect.

Chapter Twenty-One

D inner with Mom and Dad was subdued, each troubled with the worries of their nearby family. Conversation centered on Tom and Anna and the arrangements they'd yet to make for Melody's funeral. Her body had not yet been released by the coroner but was expected to be soon. The coroner and the only mortuary in the Owens Valley were one and the same. Anna was in charge of the religious ceremony of the funeral, while Tom handled logistics. Both felt it necessary to have a role in their daughter's services in Wesley's absence. Dad and Mom had both helped and ironed out a dignified, respectful ceremony.

I gave them a synopsis of Blaine's fishing expedition. Both my parents liked Blaine—he was a personable guy, after all. But their loyalty was to me, so they had little to say about the circumstances. Thankfully, neither lowered themselves to disparage him. They did, however, briefly get excited about the possibility of having Rusty around. I told them not to anticipate it as it wasn't likely that Blaine would give up his bargaining chip so early in the game. I prepared them for further hijinks from my ex-husband. I'd seen his mischief-making to others while we were married and had chalked it up to pranks. But now, I realize it was more a shade of bullying. And now *I* was the focus.

The idea of going back to him was out of the question. He'd lied and cheated on me, squandered his—our —money, and harassed those from whom he wanted something.

My phone chimed a cheery tune from my jeans pocket. Not recognizing the caller's phone number, I debated whether to answer.

I gave in and pushed the green button. "This is Sarah Murray."

"Miz Murray, I'm calling because Libby asked me to get in touch."

My pulse raced. The police chief's son. "Yes, thanks for getting back to me. I have some questions I'd like to ask if you're up to it."

He paused. "Can I meet you on East Line past the Research Center after sunset?"

"The White Mountain Research Station?" Why the secretiveness?

"It's called the Research Center now."

"Of course. I'll be in a white Camry."

Chapter Twenty-Two

E ast Line Street stretched out into the desert for miles to the White Mountain Research Center. The facility was a university-level field research facility of the University of California, Los Angeles. Scientists from all over the world used the facility for varying earth sciences. It was a gated compound of several acres containing labs, dorms, and offices.

The road twisted around the base of the mountain range and became Eastside Road, eventually connecting to Warm Springs Road. Warm Springs dead-ended at Highway 395. It was about as far east as a vehicle could travel. There was no traffic.

I drove over the cattle guard east of the Research Center until my headlights shone on a spot with enough of a shoulder to park off the road. This was all open range. Only the Research Center had fences out here. I could see the road for miles, a flat asphalt and gravel ribbon spread along the valley floor. The breeze carried the sound of crickets chirping, and nearby a hawk swooped to the sand to snatch an evening snack. It looked like a rodent of some sort, with spindly legs clawing at the air.

I parked under a dead tree, turned off the engine, and got out. The silence overwhelmed me as I leaned against the car. Even having grown up here, after being away for ten years with traffic, sirens, aircraft, and general noise, the silence would take some getting used to. I looked up. The stars shone brighter here and more abundantly. Southern California light pollution masked what I could see now. Viewing the stars was something I missed down south.

Headlights from the west caught my attention. The evening breeze had carried away any motor noise. This should be my guy. I wondered how far I should press him. What information would he have? At this point, I didn't even know his name, just that he was the police chief's son.

Sound finally caught up with the light, and a 1980s vintage Dodge truck pulled up behind my Camry. I stayed where I was, waiting. He was clearly reluctant as he took several minutes of fussing around in the front seat. Finally, he got out. A lean, clean-shaven teenage boy. He mashed a brown cowboy hat over his crew cut and ambled toward me.

I straightened. "Are you Libby's friend?"

He nodded.

I extended my hand. "I'm Sarah Murray."

He shook it, and I felt the calloused hands of a working cowboy. "And you are?"

He sucked in a lungful of air. "My name's Cameron Scherwin."

"The police chief's son."

He nodded. "You're the eye doctor's daughter."

I smiled. He'd done some homework. "Libby's upset

about Melody's death. We all are. She was my cousin but more like a sister."

He nodded. Pulling teeth would be easier.

"I'm looking into what happened." The darkness had descended and was absolute. No moon tonight. I couldn't see the expression on his face, so I tried to read his body language. He was tense, but it was understandable. For whatever reason—I hoped to find out—he wanted to keep this meeting secret. Secrets carry built-in tension, in addition to the reason for the mystery. I continued, "Libby told me that you and Melody spent time together."

He grunted with indignation, and I jumped to clarify my statement. "She didn't tell me why. Just that you found Melody a good listener."

"She was."

In the courtroom, some of the best attorneys used silence to encourage their witnesses to talk. This was the tactic I used here. I glanced toward town, noting headlights in the distance.

"I trusted Melody. She never told anyone."

Silence. The headlights grew closer. Someone going to the research station, maybe?

"You're a lot like her, you know." He shifted, and in the faint starlight, I saw his young face. His clear-eyed, pleasant appearance hid a tortured soul.

"I'll take that as a compliment."

"It was meant to be. She listened, really listened. She wasn't one to interrupt or force her opinions on me."

"I always thought she could've been a therapist or counselor. But she was surprisingly good at whatever she chose to do."

A bat flew past, then another. It was their dinnertime, and mosquitos were on the menu. I shivered. The evening was cooling down. The headlights drove past the research station's gate. The car would pass us in a moment.

"You want to know what was going on between us?"

The way he said it made an alarm bell go off. Was Melody romantically involved with this teenager? I braced myself.

An unmarked, unmistakably law enforcement car slowed to a stop parallel to us. Cameron's sharp intake of breath compounded my alarm. Who was this? His father, of course.

Leaving the car running, a potbellied middle-aged man with an air of swagger got out. In a gesture exactly like Cameron's, he slipped on his straw cowboy hat. He wore a uniform shirt with jeans. Thankfully, I saw no sidearm.

His square chin nodded to Cameron. "You. Get home."

"Yessir." Cameron avoided looking my way and made for his truck. He started it up, made a U-turn, and drove back into town, loose gravel ricocheting off the truck fenders.

I stayed where I was. Blocked in by the chief's car, it would've been awkward to leave. He clearly had something to say. So, I leaned against my car and looped my arms across my chest. Classic resistant body language, but I didn't care. This guy smelled like a bully, and I didn't like bullies.

"You're the eye doctor's kid, ain't ya?"

"Yes, Sarah Murray. And you're the police chief." I waited for the courtesy of his name.

"Yep." He looked around and slipped a toothpick into his mouth.

I sniffed. He'd seen too many *Cool Hand Luke* movies.

The guy was trying to act like a powerful man when in actuality, he was just a big fish in a little pond. Even so, this was going to be unpleasant.

"Well, Sarah Murray. You need to mind your own business."

"This is my business."

"Nope, it ain't." The toothpick bobbed in his full lips. The starlight illuminated his pale, fleshy face. "You're messing with my family now, and that ain't a good thing."

"Your son has information about a murder, sir. The murder of my cousin. My family."

"Cameron doesn't know nuthin'."

"You're wrong." I straightened, hands on my hips. "And you call yourself a law enforcement officer. There's a murderer loose in this community, and you're blocking attempts to identify him."

"By you? Are you kidding? You're just some piece of fluff from the flat lands with no authority or training to be questioning people."

"If I don't, who will? Sheriff Dorsey?" I sniffed at the idea.

"Little lady, that homicide is in his jurisdiction. He runs the investigation the way he thinks it should be done."

"Like arresting Wesley Charters? That was a lame move. He'll be lucky if Wesley doesn't sue him."

He pulled the toothpick out of his mouth and tossed it away. "That's not for you to say."

This was going all wrong. I didn't like this guy, but I didn't need to. I wanted to talk to his son. Clearly, his son wouldn't be available to me without his father's permission. I should take it down a notch.

I exhaled and tried to relax my posture. "Look, we

don't need to be adversaries. All I want to do is talk to your son…"

"Why? So you can accuse him?"

"No, no. I don't see him as any threat or aggressor in this mess. I'm just trying to account for the last hours of my cousin's life."

"Yeah?"

"Melody had left from visiting her mother, Anna Gibson, at 7:00 p.m. At 8:15 p.m., her brother-in-law, Jake Charters, arrived at the house for a visit. He opened the car door, and his dog ran off, chasing a rabbit. Melody and Jake went in opposite directions looking for the dog. An hour later, she's lying in the desert, bleeding from a head wound. Then the ambulance picks her up and transports her to Northern Inyo Hospital, where she's pronounced dead at 9:30 p.m. I don't understand the gaps in time." I took a deep breath and continued. "Melody was the only one home when Jake arrived, but he had the feeling she'd just said goodbye to a visitor. I think Cameron came to see her then. Would you allow me to ask him about that?"

He grunted.

"We can make an appointment to meet in your office —your turf—if you like. You can be there as well." I wasn't sure how forthcoming Cameron would be in front of his father, but I had to try. "I really have no intention of harming your son. He seems like a nice young man. He might've seen something that would lead to the identity of the killer."

The chief sighed. After thirty seconds, he said, "Tomorrow morning. Eight o'clock. My office."

He whirled around, got back into his car, flipped a U-turn, and drove off.

Chapter Twenty-Three

Cameron surely didn't feel any better after our meeting, but I was cautiously optimistic as I drove back into town. Eliminating Cameron from the suspect list would help. Talking to him also gave me a means to help Wesley, Libby, and, indirectly, Cameron. We'd see what revelations tomorrow would bring.

Faint headlights appeared in my rearview mirror. Cameron and his father had left before me, so I knew it wasn't them. I hadn't passed parked cars. There was the off chance it was a student or scientist from the Research Center. Knowing most of the staff were basically transient, here for the summer term, it wouldn't likely be someone looking for a party.

It could also be my mystery tail.

I decided to find out. Driving west past the Bishop Creek Canal, I approached the residential outskirts of town. To my left sat homes and apartments, but to my right was a steel structure housing a locksmith and storage business. I'd been there before with Dad and recalled the layout. Sodium vapor lighting was on but didn't reach the corners I expected to be in.

I swerved into the lot, fighting the impulse to sit on the brakes until I got out of view from East Line Street. I pulled up into a dark corner, jumped out of the car, and ran to the canal side of the property. If I was being followed, I expect the sedan would motor into the lot after me. By circling around, I hoped to sneak up behind and take a picture of the license plate. I'd hold on to it, but if I had to... what would I do? Give it to Jake? Why would this car make me feel in jeopardy? Being followed isn't a normal occurrence. What if...?

I'd give it to Kelly and 'fess up. Tell him I've been snooping around town and asking people questions. No doubt I'd get an earful of 'leave it to the professionals.' If I left it to the sheriff, they'd stick with the easy solution —Wesley, the guy already in jail for the crime. I was fairly sure there wasn't any further investigation. That didn't work for me, so I'd keep up my inquiries, even if it had to be subtle.

I heard the car. He was at the canal, then twenty feet into the parking lot. I moved around the building, thankful it was empty, stopping at the end of the fence. I peered around it and watched the dark sedan follow my trail into the lot. It stopped. I saw his head swivel with confusion. He saw the car but not me.

Walking purposefully but quietly, I moved in behind his car and took the picture. The driver's head snapped up as he looked around. Settling on me, he wheeled the car around, tires squealing, and shot out of the lot.

I got enough of a glimpse to identify him—male in his late forties, looked Hispanic, bald, with no beard or mustache. He looked like a cop.

Pleased with my ingenuity, I texted Jake the license plate number and driver description. I ended the text with, *Meet me at the sub.*

Chapter Twenty-Four

Jake wasn't happy with what I'd done. His text in reply said, *We will talk about this.*

I was sure Kelly would chew me out too. While I didn't relish the confrontations, I wanted to be sure Kelly had the info. I had no idea what the guy in the dark sedan had to do with anything. But his activity was suspicious, and in view of Melody's murder and Wesley's arrest, I had to take this seriously.

It was after hours, but the lights were on inside the substation. Kelly had said he would be working for the next three days, so I texted him to let me in.

He locked the door behind me and said, "What are you doing out at night?"

I didn't want to repeat myself, so to buy time until Jake got here, I smiled and thought up a coy remark. "Does a girl have to have a reason to visit an old friend?"

"No, but that's not what you're doing, is it, Sarah?"

"Okay, maybe there is an ulterior motive."

A banging rattled the front door. Jake, I hoped.

Kelly unlocked the door, and Jake barged through and

past the deputy. The frown Jake wore told me I was in for a double scolding. Arco followed, bounding in to greet me. At least someone was happy to see me. I bent to greet him with what was probably an excess of enthusiasm.

"What were you thinking?" Jake squared off with me, his face darkening. "You don't know what you're messing with. You could've been hurt, or worse."

"Wait a minute," Kelly shouted over my retort. "Wait a minute." He pulled my forearm to face him. "What have you done now?"

A low, ominous growl vibrated from Arco. Jake issued a terse command, and the dog sat immediately. As for Jake, it was just like a man to take another man's side without hearing what I had to say. "Saving your butt from a false arrest suit, Kelly McSorley. That's what." Kelly's eyes were already wide from Arco's threat. They stayed that way. "You don't think Wesley killed Melody. I know it. I saw it in your face when Dorsey told you to hook him up."

"What? You're snooping around?"

"Worse than that," Jake cut in. "She's stopping strangers and taking pictures of their license plates."

"This guy's been following me since that night. I had to…"

"No, you didn't." both men said in unison.

Holy cow. They were ganging up on me. I shrugged. "Somebody had to do something." I looked at Kelly. "You're so worried about your job that you'll let an innocent man go to prison." I turned to Jake. "And you… you're not proactive at all. Your innocent brother is rotting in jail, and you're feeding his cats."

Kelly's hands flew up defensively. "You don't know what you're talking about. Nor do you know what you're doing." He slapped Jake on the shoulder. "He's right. You could get in big trouble, like messing with an investigation."

"Is there really an investigation, Kelly? Or has Dorsey closed the book on Wesley Charters?" I was sure I knew the answer.

"Okay, just a minute here. Let's just cool down." Jake's voice deepened. Maybe he saw my reasoning. I felt the temperature in the room cool. "I believe Sarah has some information that you should know." His gaze shot to Kelly. "Even if the case is closed, it isn't. Is it?"

Kelly took a deep breath and rebooted. "Let's sit down and list all the information you've gotten."

Relief flooded through me. I was going to get my chance. Even if Dorsey shut the investigation down, my information might point to the real killer. I pulled a dusty whiteboard from the back of the room. Kelly handed me a dry-erase marker, and I began my diagram. Melody left her mother's house at 7:00 p.m. She drove home and—this is my theory, and I hope to prove it tomorrow morning—met with a young man for counseling. She was found at about 8:50 p.m. and transported to Northern Inyo Hospital at 9:00 p.m. She was pronounced deceased at 9:30 p.m.

I sketched an outline of a pair of suspects. I began with the church organist, Vernelle Kearney. "She had a crush on Wesley and felt Melody wasn't good enough for him. The second suspect was Reginald Bateau, the heir to the Boulangerie. According to Libby, in an effort to put Layers out of business, he spread rumors about an unsanitary kitchen and its imminent failure. When none of the rumors gained any traction, he offered to buy Melody out. She refused, of course, giving Bateau motive to get rid of her. There's a third possibility in the clown who was trailing me. He was an unknown quantity."

Kelly had a question. "What about this mystery young man?

"I'm sure we can rule him out. Like I said, I'll know more tomorrow."

"Then what about Libby? She's been in trouble before. Is there a motive for her...?"

"Not a chance." I was certain. "It was in her best interest to keep Melody alive. Mel had become a mentor to Libby, kept her out of trouble, and tutored her to the honor roll. She graduates next week, which is what she and Melody were working for."

Kelly twisted the microphone cable on his portable radio as he considered my answer. It was a habit I'd seen in the bored courtroom bailiffs often. "Who else have you talked to?"

"I've only been in town two days."

Kelly flashed an embarrassed smile. "Two days, and you've done more than me."

"The two of us have jobs to protect." Jake had settled down and was thinking things through. "Maybe there's a way to do both."

I sighed. "You can't bring Vernelle Kearney or Reginald Bateau in for interviews. Dorsey would get wind and wouldn't stand for it."

Kelly agreed, looking at Jake. "He's the kind of guy who'd call your chief and tell him you're interfering."

"We need to think of a way to talk to each of them in a place that's quiet, secure, and unobtrusive." Jake scratched Arco's ear.

"That's easy," I volunteered. "Layers. It's all three of those. All we have to do is keep the front shades closed, and no one can look in." I drew a simple floor plan on the whiteboard. The kitchen and the front counter—two rooms. With two interviewers and two suspects, we had one set of logistics in hand.

"We need a plan to get them in the shop and a strategy to get answers." Jake took this as seriously as I did. I was pleased to have the cooperation of these two professional lawmen.

Then, a tiny tingle of suspicion waggled in the back of my mind. Jake had been in the Wilkerson desert looking for Arco. No one saw him, hence, no alibi. I pushed it away as I listened to the two men brainstorm how they were going to get Kearney and Bateau to the bakery.

I pulled out my phone and scrolled to the photos. "What about the license plate?"

Kelly plopped in front of a computer and asked me to repeat it. Seconds later, he looked up, from Jake to me. "It's confidential."

Jake nodded. "I'm not surprised. I'm betting he's a PI, either a retired cop or still on the job."

The possibilities ran through my head—a PI hired by someone keeping tabs on my amateur inquiries? Who had money for that? Bateau? Probably. Kearney? No way.

Kelly squinted against an imminent disaster. "What about your ex, Sarah? Would he do something like this?"

"I don't think so." The room was silent as I reconsidered my answer. Would Blaine have someone follow me? To what end? Where would he find the money for that? Oh, the house closed today. There wasn't much profit but enough to fund this enterprise. I shook my head. "At least, I don't believe so. For the life of me, I can't imagine what he'd want to find."

Arco's deep-brown eyes watched me as I contemplated what I'd just said.

Chapter Twenty-Five

At five minutes to eight the next morning, I stood on the front doorstep of the Bishop Police Department. I pushed the intercom button and waited. After identifying myself, the dispatcher buzzed me in and said to wait for the chief. I scanned the lobby photographs until I found one with the chief's name—Frank Scherwin.

My phone read eight o'clock when an interior door swung open. Cameron followed his father into the business office. Frank Scherwin buzzed open the security door to let me in. He showed me into his office, Cameron following me this time.

The elder Scherwin stood behind his desk, a cup of coffee steaming beside a stack of folders. His face was sober when he reached across to shake my hand. "Frank Scherwin, as you might have guessed."

A little surprised, I glanced at Cameron, whose solemn gaze met mine.

"Why do I have the feeling I'm going to be ambushed?"

Frank sat and motioned for Cameron and me to take the pair of chairs opposite his desk. "Not at all, Ms. Murray. As a matter of fact, I believe we owe you an apology."

"Apology?" Stunned, all I could do was repeat the word.

Cameron turned to me to explain. "Yes. Dad and I have not been honest with each other about all this..." He swung his arm to encompass a murder, a below-the-radar relationship, and who knows what else. "When he got home last night, well, we talked. We talked about the things that are going wrong in our lives and damaging our family."

Frank took a sip of coffee while Cameron spoke, then added, "Your honesty to me last night was an eye-opener. I realized that Cameron isn't the enemy, nor are you. On my way home, I had time to think about what you said. I'm aboard. I want to help as much as I can to find out who killed Melody Charters. My only stipulation is that I'd rather not make an enemy of Stan Dorsey. We're old friends, and I'd hate to jeopardize that and our working relationship."

"So," Cameron smiled for the first time. "Ask your questions."

I'd had no idea what to expect this morning, but I certainly didn't expect this. I considered the questions I had and decided I'd jump right in.

"When your dad showed up last night, you were about to tell me what your association with Melody was."

Cameron picked at a fingernail, then straightened in the chair. "First, I don't believe her husband murdered her."

My chest was tight. "He didn't do it, but he doesn't

have an alibi that he can reveal, so I must find out the truth. It's the only way to free him."

Cameron huffed, knowing he was treading on sensitive territory. He decided on the sacrifice. "Libby and I are tight."

I glanced at Frank to see his reaction. "It's fine. We talked it out last night. No more secrets."

"Thanks for your honesty." Exhaling my relief, I faced the son. "Now, tell me why that was a secret."

"It was about my dad." At my nod, he continued. "Well, he hates Libby, her father, and the rest of the family. I guess one of them was involved with some big-time theft from a business years ago. Her mom committed suicide, but my dad didn't believe she took the money. It was his case when he was a detective. Libby's dad was a real jerk about it all, and my dad never forgot. He thinks... thought... the whole family is tainted."

"There's more to this, isn't there?" Ancient history is always remembered in small towns, and Bishop was no different. But holding a grudge for generations was something else.

"Yeah." He kicked at the desk with the toe of his cowboy boot. "Libby and her dad don't get along—at all. In fact, they can't be in the same room. But for my dad, it's Libby herself. She got into trouble a few years ago. She fell in with a bunch of idiots, got herself all tatted up, rings in her nose, and all kinds of stupid stuff." He shook his head at the nonsense of it. "But she's straightened out. Melody helped her believe in herself, and she's been doing *really* good. She's on the honor roll at her school." Libby had told me this. She'd been sent to a continuation school because of chronic absenteeism and behavioral issues. Melody had been one of her high school teachers. Even after her transfer to the continuation school, Melody hadn't given up on her. A few months after Layers was up and running, Melody brought Libby aboard like an apprenticeship. With Melody's involvement, Libby turned herself around. Not only that, but she'd excelled. "But my dad thought she's a bad influence on me."

"What did Melody say about this?"

"She told me to give my dad time. Libby was doing so well at the bakery that Melody was giving her extra projects. She's been doing a lot of the baking. Melody said Libby would prove to everyone that she was responsible and all that boring stuff." He met my gaze, his face drawn in fierce determination. "In the meantime, we'd still have to sneak around, keep it on the down-low. And I hated that. I want to be able to take my girl for coffee or out to a movie."

Some would've suggested to have an intervention with Cameron's dad, but Melody's advice sounded more rational. It made more sense that he'd trust Libby's behavior changes if he saw them instead of being hammered with reasons to believe in her.

"I understand. I think Melody's advice is sound. If he can see Libby being responsible, he'll trust it." This made me think of Layers, where Libby shined. Maybe she and I should consider opening for a few hours with Libby's baking skills, and I could work the cash register. Since it was counter service only, no waitstaff was needed. I wondered if Libby would be up for it. Of course, we'd have to get the go-ahead from Wesley as well as Tom and Anna just to be on the safe side.

"There's one more thing."

Uh oh. One more thing he waited to tell me last.

"I was with Melody the night she was killed."

Even expecting this bad news, I couldn't contain my sharp intake of breath. "Go on."

Embarrassed at this part of the story, his head bowed. "Dad and I had another blowout, and I was mad at him. I came out to Melody's house to calm down."

He glanced at my face and saw my eyes widening with dread.

He rushed to explain, "But she was alive when I last saw her. Believe me, ma'am."

I searched his face for the truth. In the bright morning light, I had no trouble reading him. "What time did you leave?" This felt right.

"Oh, about eight o'clock. The PD dispatcher called me because the north fence on our ranch was down and the cattle got out."

"There will be a record of the phone call, then."

Frank nodded. "I already checked this morning. It's timestamped on the computer. There's no way anyone could go into the program and change the time."

I released a breath I didn't know I'd been holding. The time of Melody's assault was after eight o'clock, estimated to be 8:30 to 8:45 p.m. Cameron had an alibi. Thanking God for this small mercy. I liked Cameron, and he was important to Libby. "As far as Melody's advice, you're smart to pay attention to her. It looks like you've found a conclusion to your troubles sooner than you thought."

He smiled at his dad, who gave him a broad smile back.

Chapter Twenty-Six

I spent the next hour honing a proposition for Libby. I'd see Wesley tomorrow at the jail, but this morning, I was off to catch Anna and Tom. Although I didn't know the protocols, it seemed the right thing to ask for their blessing.

Over coffee at their kitchen table, Anna jumped at the idea. Tom held back, thinking the business end through before offering his approval.

Anna gripped her husband's hand. "Tom, this is exactly what Melody would want. She put months of energy into that young girl. She'd want us to continue otherwise, all that time could be lost. *She* would be lost."

"Who would run the business end?"

"For now, I would. If we can continue to make a profit, we'll hire someone for the counter service."

"What about profits?" Tom's jaw set with indecision.

"Any profit will go back into the business, including salary for staff, except for me."

"And don't you have a job waiting for you?"

"The background check isn't complete yet. I was told

it would be done by mid-June. That's two weeks away. Then the county has the pre-employment checklist to complete. That should be another week. By then, we should have a handle on whether this will work without Melody." The finality of the last few words sank into all of us. "I have a plan, but I don't want to give you details until I'm sure I can make it work."

"What's the alternative?" Anna looked from Tom to me. "Close down? Sell the business? All her tools?"

"She has a bank loan that needs to be paid as well as supply invoices. If we sell, there will barely be enough to cover the expenses." I had no idea if they considered Wesley's legal expenses. I let that be for now.

Tom squinted with his doubtful smile. "You're asking us to trust you, Sarah."

"Yes, I am."

"Tom?" Anna's gaze riveted on her husband.

After a moment, Tom said, "Legally, I don't know where we stand. Wesley's future is uncertain. I don't think Mel had a will. If she did, I doubt she'd leave anything to us. We..." he swallowed hard. "We were supposed to go first."

Anna pushed the heels of her hands against her eyes. The moment grew tense but passed when she straightened in her chair. "I trust Sarah. I want to give her a chance to fulfill our daughter's dream."

Tom sucked in a mouthful of air and reached a hand across the table. "All right, Sarah. You've got the bakery. Let's give it until you start work at the courthouse, then reassess."

I couldn't ask for more. I gripped his hand tightly. "Deal."

Chapter Twenty-Seven

My next stop was Libby's house. She was at school, of course. But Grant said she'd be home early today, sometime in the next hour. I returned to Layers and used the time to study the books. Mel had shown a profit but still owed on the bank loan. It looked to me like if Libby and I worked the rest of this month and next to pay the bills, Layers might have a chance to survive. Libby would have to waive her salary for a short time, but then we could look to the future.

I texted Libby to meet me at Layers when school was over. I'd left the back door open as I had her keys. In thirty minutes, I heard a motorscooter pull up. That would be Libby. I stood at the doorway, watching her pull off her helmet and backpack.

Her face flushed from the exhilarating ride from school, and I hoped, anticipation of a future here. Where most teens would be slow to come to work, Libby was tense with excitement.

"Come in and sit down. We need to talk. I've got a kettle on for your tea."

Her smile reflected her gratitude, and minutes later, I slid a mug of tea across the baker's worktable. Faint whisps of flour colored the surface, but otherwise, it was immaculate.

Libby dipped a honey-laden spoon into the tea and stirred. Her eyes followed the tiny whirlpool in the mug. "You gonna fire me? Close up shop?"

"No. I don't want to close this place up." Admiring the stainless equipment, tools, and ovens, I couldn't imagine letting my cousin down. She'd put her life into this place.

"Libby, remember you told me how Melody saved you?"

Libby nodded.

"I think it's our turn to do the same for her."

Libby shook her head with doubt. "What do you mean? We can't save her."

"No, we can't, but we can save her dream."

"What're you talking about?"

I held out my hand, motioning to the room. "This. This place was her dream. It's what she wanted to do for the rest of her life." I took a deep breath and spilled the rest of Mel's dream. "You had quite an impact on her, you know. The way you turned your life around and inspired her to do more than bake pies."

Astonished, Libby sat motionless, listening.

"The week before she passed, she started talking about making the bakery more than just desert desserts. She wanted to help marginalized, at-risk youth, to give them the chance you had. She was working on making this place a nonprofit for this purpose."

When she could speak, she asked, "Really? I did that?"

"Yes, you inspired Melody to do for others, just as she

has all her life. Until now, I didn't think this place had room for that vision."

"So, how can we save her dream?" I saw the gears turning. Melody was right to trust this kid. She had creativity, energy, and drive.

"First, we need to open for business. We must make enough money to make the bank loan, rent, and buy supplies. For that, we need income. I thought we could open for, say, four hours on weekday mornings for people going to work. Friday nights when tourists head north to Mammoth and Sunday afternoons when they return down south will be high traffic times. We must plan for that with fresh baked goods and staffing."

Her jaw dropped and stayed down until I finished talking. Then all she could say was, "Whoa."

"It looks like it's up to you and me. Do you have any thoughts on how to do all this?"

"Hell..."

I put up my hand, stopping her. "No cussing. I have the same rules as my cousin. No profanity."

"Yes, ma'am." Her head dipped in an enthusiastic nod. "Okay, what about this... I'll do the baking." she squinted at me.

"I was hoping you'd say that."

"Good. It's what I love to do anyway. I'll work early Monday through Friday afternoon to catch the north-bound traffic with fresh goods. Saturday we can open for sales only, then Sunday..."

"Sunday, after church..."

"Uh huh, after church." She gave me a curious glance. I didn't imagine she went to church, but I wanted to remind her that people did, especially here in Bishop. I did. Who knows, maybe she'd come with me someday. Without Wesley, I questioned whether services would be held. I had to trust that the business office would find a substitute. But that wasn't my concern.

Her voice rising with excitement, she continued. "Sunday, I'll come in and bake for the southbound tourists. We can set up a curbside drive-up service with coffee and pie for the road. People can text in their orders. Because we're on Main Street, they're on their way out of town anyway."

Astonished at her imagination, I had to smile. "Great ideas. How to order? The website has to be updated to allow for orders and payment." I shrugged. "I can do some, but that tech knowledge is beyond me. Do you know anyone trustworthy?"

She pursed her lips, thinking. "There are a few kids at school who have the smarts. I'm not sure they'll help. But I can ask."

"Good. Do it soon. Right after you graduate Monday night."

"Right." Suddenly, Libby was silent, all energy contained inside instead of spilling out her pores. "We'll make this work. Layers is Melody's legacy."

"No, you're wrong. You're her legacy, Libby. Not the brick-and-mortar business, but your life. You and anyone Layers can help."

Libby's eyes dampened, as did mine.

Chapter Twenty-Eight

Preoccupied with the morning's events, I didn't see the dark sedan until I turned my Camry onto Mountain View. It continued on to West Line Street. Instead of pulling into my McLaren Lane driveway, I made a U-turn and pulled out onto West Line.

The car was parked in the dirt parking lot in front of Izaak Walton Park, across from my neighborhood. A lone occupant sat behind the wheel.

I pulled over and parked directly in front of him. I know Kelly and Jake were worried about my seemingly impulsive actions, but I wanted to confront this thorn in my side. I wanted him to go home to his wife and kids and leave me alone.

My anger built as I approached him. But he stayed behind the wheel, his face impassive. It was like he expected me.

I tapped his window, and he scrolled it down. He glared but remained silent.

"You," I started. "Why are you doing this?"

He looked at my car blocking his egress and said, "Good question."

"Well... tell me why."

He shrugged. "The pay's good. The work is easy. Until you came along."

"You know what I mean."

His face scrunched in consternation. "I can't tell you who's paying the bill, if that's what you're after."

"That's exactly what I want to know. Who's paying you to follow me?"

He slipped a toothpick into his mouth. "You honestly don't know?"

"It's Blaine, my ex-husband, right?"

"I just said I can't tell you..."

"Can you tell me if I'm wrong?"

He smiled. He had a nice smile, but that didn't make him a good person. "Try me."

"Blaine Hoffman."

This time he grinned.

Bingo. That jerk I used to be married to was having me followed. "What was he looking for? I'm not cheating or stealing..."

"I know, I know..."

Indignation rose in my chest. "You know? Well then, why are you doing this?"

He motioned me away from his car door. When he was out, he leaned on the fender and pulled out the toothpick, tossing it into the weeds. "I did some checking on you."

I didn't like where this was going.

"You see, I'm a retired policeman, name's Bernal. I can smell a dirtbag from a mile off. It's a survival mechanism called profiling." He waved the thought away. "I got nothing even off-color from you. But your ex is a real stinker."

"Tell me about it."

"I can't. Believe me, I wish I could, but I have to maintain some standards. I've overstepped by talking to you. But you should know that I'm no danger to you, physically or financially." The emphasis he put on the last word put me on guard. Financially. Hmm.

"Well, thank you," I said as he got back into his car. "I guess."

Chapter Twenty-Nine

"What? Again?" Jake's angry tone made me want to hang up. "You're asking for trouble, Sarah."

"Stop yelling. I had enough of that from Blaine. Just stop."

"Okay," he muttered. "You're right. I have no business telling you what to do."

"Jake, I know you're trying to help, but I know what's going on at the moment I decide to do something."

"Okay," he said again. "You want to meet for an early dinner? You can tell me what he said."

"That would be great. We also need to set a time to visit Wesley tomorrow."

"Sure. Let's meet at the Dagwood Diner in Cottonwood Plaza. You know it?" I thought hamburgers would be to his taste, and Dagwood's served up a juicy, flavorful burger. They were very popular, although I usually had a Cobb salad. "Let's meet there at six." Meeting at the restaurant had more of a business feel than that of a date. I didn't want Jake to get the wrong idea.

And what idea was that? I liked him. I might even

allow myself to become 'interested' in him when all this drama has been concluded, and I had time to heal from a decade of Blaine. But for now, I wanted to keep it strictly business.

"Deal." he said. "I've gotta take this call. See you then."

I spent the few hours until dinner going through the books at the bakery, calculating debits and credits, talking to the bank, and looking for a local business attorney. I had little resolved when I pulled into a parking space in front of Dagwood's.

I was shocked to see Wesley standing in front of the restaurant with Jake. Wesley looked pale and like he needed a long rest but otherwise presentable.

I gripped him in a hug, noticing how frail he felt when he hugged back. "Wesley, it's so good to see you here. What happened to get you out?"

He gave a crooked smile, like the grin on his brother's lips. The genetics had stamped both men. "Dad hired some attorney from LA who shook the Inyo County DA's tree. He's reviewing the case now."

"They released you on your own recognizance?" This was unheard of in a capital crime.

He shrugged, not knowing the technicalities. "Dad said my attorney threatened a false arrest lawsuit because the case is short on evidence other than circumstantial. I don't have a court date or anything yet. The lawyer said he'd take care of it and let me know."

I'd love to see what evidence Dorsey put forth. As far as I knew, Kelly wrote the report, and he wasn't sold on Wesley's guilt. "Well, thank God for that."

Jake ushered us in. After a word with the short Latinx server, we were shown to a table in a corner. I thought it a good move as I wasn't sure how welcome Wesley would be in public. We settled in and chatted until we'd ordered. As the server walked away, Jake leaned into the table. "So, Wes, we have some questions that you need to answer."

Wesley rubbed his knuckles as he looked away from me. "Sarah, I wasn't sure if you'd want to see me."

Clasping his hand, I said, "I know you didn't... kill Melody."

"She's been working diligently trying to find out who did." Jake added.

It was Wesley's turn to put his hand on mine. "I hear you're taking risks to get at the truth, Sarah. Please don't."

I pushed his worries aside as my iced tea arrived. "I don't take risks that aren't calculated for safety. Don't you remember, they call me Sensible Sarah." I looked to Jake. "Speaking of which, where is Arco? At home with the cats?"

He inclined his head toward the restaurant parking lot. "He's in the car over there with the AC going full blast. He's got it pretty good right now."

"Okay, just asking."

"Let's get down to business," Jake got to the questions. "Where were you Wednesday night? Why did you cancel Bible study?"

Wesley stared at the Formica table, fingering the trim. "It's embarrassing to say."

Jake prodded. "C'mon, Wes. This is important. You need a solid alibi."

"Vernelle Kearney."

"The organist?" I looked to Jake. He didn't seem surprised.

Wesley rushed the explanation. "She called and said she had an emergency at her house. Something I had to help with. In my vanity, I thought it was a crisis of faith that only I could heal." His cheeks colored.

This made sense. I'd always figured Vernelle had lied to me. I just didn't know what or why. Now I did.

"Go on." Jake urged.

"She answered the door in tears. I thought somebody had died and she needed comfort."

"She needed comfort, all right." Jake grimaced.

"She grabbed me and wouldn't let go. Had her arms around my neck." Wesley's eyes telegraphed the defensiveness. "Really."

"What time did you arrive, and when did you leave?" Jake's gaze riveted on his brother. "This is critical, Wes."

"Right." He reached for his phone, scrolled through, and, finding what he was looking for, smiled in triumph. "Here. I was at home when she called at six forty-five. I fired off an email to the study group and drove right over. She lives on Short Street, so it wasn't more than ten minutes from our house. Say 7:00 p.m."

"How long were you there?" Jake had taken out a small tablet and jotted down notes.

Wesley traced a line above his brow with an index finger and thumb. "Um, I stayed about an hour." He fired a look at his brother. "She was upset. I tried to settle her down. We prayed together, but she was still scared that I'd tell someone."

"And now you have." Jake closed his notebook with finality. "Look, your only other choice was to stay in jail."

I had a thought. "She might not corroborate Wes's account." Thinking over what she'd told me, I decided to voice my observations. "She had unkind things to say about Melody."

Jake picked up the recollection. "She said Melody was having an affair."

"Affair?" Wesley's eyebrows lifted in surprise.

"Yeah, with some young boy—the police chief's son."

"Cameron? What would make her think that?"

I could answer that. "She was seeing him, but only for counseling. He has an ongoing family issue... that he needed guidance with."

"Oh, you're right." Wesley straightened, his face crumpling with a recollection. "She told me she had talked to him, but I didn't know why or that it was an ongoing task."

Jake added, "She also said you were probably following her."

"Oh, my Lord. I wish I had been. Then I could've stopped whoever killed her."

Chapter Thirty

My phone chimed a waiting text message at seven-thirty. From Mom, it said, *Come home now*. I tossed my portion of the dinner bill at the check and stood up. "Gotta go."

Jake and Wesley sat, seeming at a loss of what to do. "Go home, Wesley. Jake will be there with you."

"I assumed it would be part of the crime scene... that I wouldn't be allowed to..."

Jake threw more bills on the table. "It's not. They searched the place, but I've been staying there. Let's go home. You need a shower, a change of clothes, and to sleep in your own bed."

My ten-minute drive home was fraught with worry about what the urgency was for me to get home. Since Mom texted, I thought Dad might've had a medical issue. When I pulled into my driveway, I understood her insistence. Blaine was there, and she had to entertain him until I arrived. His car sat on the far end of the U-shaped driveway, a silver 2019 Audi A8 sedan.

Blaine had laughed at me when he first brought it home. "Sensible Sarah. Driving a six-year-old Toyota."

The fact that my car was paid for didn't connect with him. He liked the looks he got driving a car that cost ninety thousand dollars. He liked the respect of his colleagues in the movie industry, few of whom drove more expensive cars. He wasn't a big money earner as a location scout, not like the stars. But he felt he had a certain persona he had to display. And that meant spending money. He didn't care that I had to work extra hours to make the lease payments.

And now he was here. This was why my mother was so anxious to get me home.

I walked in the back door, being careful to put my purse away in the pantry. I didn't want to tempt fate. Blaine had cut me short before by raiding my wallet. Not this time.

Rusty ran to me, almost jumping on me but not. I knelt, hugging him and feeling his excited heartbeat. Oh, how I missed this guy! But Rusty being here could only mean one thing.

Blaine would be using him as a negotiating tool. Rusty quieted when I stood. My hand touched his head as we turned into the kitchen.

I slipped off my sweater and looked across the table at my ex-husband. "Blaine. What are you doing here?" Out of the corner of my eye, I saw Mom escape to the living room. Lucky. I made Rusty sit near me as I stood facing Blaine.

My ex-husband rose, a smile on his full lips that I used to think was sweet. Now it looked saccharine. Tall, tan, blond, and muscular, he looked like he should be on the cover of a *GQ* magazine. In his defense, his job required travel to remote, exotic, and sophisticated parts of the world. Sometimes on foot, in a taxi, all-terrain vehicle, or even on horseback, he used his camera to take pictures and videos of exterior venues. Interiors were less difficult but could be a challenge. It never snowed inside. He liked to look rugged and stylish.

Right. Being attractive helped in his profession but not at home. His charm wore off about the third year of our marriage, when I had to get a second job on weekends to pay off his debt. After ten years, there was no shine left when I found a picture of Blaine kissing his girlfriend on a mutual friend's Instagram account.

The betrayal was complete. There was no trust in the scraps of marriage that I'd held onto.

Blaine opened his hands, stepping around the table to reach for me. He wanted a hug or a kiss. I backed away, keeping my temper from rising to an unmanageable level. Through the many battles with Blaine, I'd discovered I became tongue-tied when I was angry or excited. I often wondered if Blaine pushed my buttons on purpose to get me to this state. Being lost for words reduced the confrontation time and increased the chances of me giving in.

"Blaine, why are you here?" I repeated my question.

He dropped his arms, an admission that I hadn't welcomed him. "Sarah, I came to see if you're okay. I'm worried about you."

I'll bet he worried. He needs another meal ticket.

"I read about your cousin, Melody. I'm sorry. I know you two were close."

I had nothing to say to him. I didn't even want his heartfelt condolences. My wrath evaporated. I wasn't angry anymore. I thought it might be a temporary emotion, but right now, not falling for his charisma felt like a victory. I'd been alone for the past several years.

His travel kept him gone for weeks at a time. When he returned, he often was at meetings, studios, the office, or a myriad of other places instead of home. I'd learned to be alone and enjoy it. I found it preferable to the roller-coaster of emotions that always existed in his current moment.

"You are spying on me." I said, delighting in the fact that I was on to his shenanigans. I wondered why he would spend money to hire a private investigator. What in the world did he think he'd find out?

He lifted his shoulders in his best little-boy innocent shrug. "C'mon home with me, baby. Rusty misses you." He leaned over to Rusty and ruffled his head. "I miss you."

"I'm not your baby. If Rusty misses me so much, let me keep him. It makes more sense anyway with all the travel you do."

"I couldn't do that, Ba... Sarah. I need Rusty for company."

That poor dog. Condemned to loneliness with short bursts of intense, needy affection in between. I wanted Rusty more than ever. But I knew Blaine, and if I said I wanted it, he'd hold it back and claim it as his.

"I can't believe you drove five hours to sit in my parents' kitchen wallowing in self-pity. You knew I wouldn't come back. Why did you bother?"

He tipped his head in supplication like he'd seen heroes do in a thousand movies. "Because I still love you."

This was getting tedious. I went to the coffee pot and poured myself a cup. Blaine drank tea. I didn't offer any because I didn't want him to stay a second longer. "Blaine, it's time you realized this marriage is over. We are done, *kaput, finis*. The quicker you realize that and move on to another romance, the better off you'll be."

"But Sarah, I'm serious..."

I found his sunglasses on the table next to his ball cap. I handed both to him. "Here you go. Leave. Take Rusty and go home. Spend some time with a dog who's more loyal to you than you are to him."

I pushed him out the back door. Rusty stayed by my side. Blaine had to grab his collar and drag him out. I switched on the driveway lights to illuminate his way to his expensive Audi—alone.

There, at the edge of darkness, sat a dark sedan. *Bernal?* I wondered why he was there. I assumed Blaine would've ended their contract once my ex had contacted me.

I was wrong. Why was he watching me?

Chapter Thirty-One

I slept the sleep of the dead. One of my nagging anxieties was gone. With a heart lighter than it had been in weeks, I showered, ate a light breakfast, hugged my mom and dad, then left. On my way to the bakery, I thought about last night.

Blaine appearing out of the blue had resulted in an unexpected blessing. He came to plead his case to get back together. For me, seeing him had the opposite effect. I knew for sure that our relationship was over. Certain I was better off without him, I felt able to plan a future that didn't include him. Finally.

So, I had several items on my list that were important. Wesley was out of jail and in less danger of going back now that he had an attorney who knew what he was doing. As far as finding out who killed Melody, that would always be high on my priorities, but I also had to focus on Layers and the plans that Libby and I were fashioning. I wanted to get Layers off to a good start. By then, I hoped the county courtroom job would be open. From there, I'd look for some stability. I wanted to build my bank account to be able to buy a home of my own. After all, I was thirty-six, *waaaay* too old to be living with my parents.

Sometime in the future, I'd look at another relationship. Next time, I'd look with less glare and more clarity.

It was late enough in the morning that Layers was quiet, no one around. I'd encouraged Libby to attend her senior class picnic today. She'd been looking forward to it, and I couldn't see any reason to deny her the pleasure of enjoying the last days of high school.

I hung my purse on a hook by the door and stood in the middle of the kitchen. The shades in the front of the store were still drawn, but I wanted light in the kitchen. I opened the shades on the windows at the back door and thought about what to do first.

A business plan. I pulled out Melody's laptop and found the file that contained business information. Scrolling through the file names, I selected "Layers Business Plan November 2022." I paged through it until I came to the page titled Business Competitors.

The only business listed was Boulangerie.

A firm tapping at the back door diverted my attention. I stood and saw Reginald Bateau glaring through the window. With his pointy nose more resembling a beak, I half expected him to squawk.

As it was, he groused about waiting too long at the back door. "You made me wait. That's bad for customer service."

"Hello to you, too, Reginald." I almost slipped and called him 'Reggie-baby.' "What brings you down south of Line Street?"

Dressed in a yellow polo shirt and khakis, he looked like he was on his way to the golf course instead of trying to intimidate me. As much as he tried to, he never appeared dangerous to me.

He sniffled with a squint of disdain, then squared himself. Maybe he figured I wasn't the kind to be bullied. He was right. "You'll have to pardon me. Retail runs in my blood."

"Your more polite approach is welcome."

He suppressed a smirk and looked me in the eye. "I've heard a nasty rumor that you're going to keep Layers open. Is this true?"

The speed with which news traveled in this small town took me aback. But only for a second. I thought about all the people I'd spoken to in the past few days, city permits, the bank loan officers, food service companies. I shouldn't have been surprised.

I leaned against the worktable. "That's the plan for now."

"…'For now?' Does this mean you'll be selling, or shutting down in the future?"

"Don't waste your concern on me, Reginald. We're operating day-to-day."

Reginald looped his arms across his chest. "I can make this go easier for you, Sarah."

"I doubt it."

"No, hear me out." He tried his best to sound reasonable but came across as a whiny, spoiled child. "I'd like to buy this place." He glanced around the room, doubt casting a shadow over his face.

"It's not for sale, Reginald."

Realizing he was losing any ground he'd imagined he had, he moved toward me. I stepped away. "Partners, then." he said. "Boulangerie can do the bread and Layers desserts and pastries. You can open the café in front that Melody had planned."

The thought of collaborating with this snake sent chills through me. "No." I wondered why he felt so strongly. "Does your mother feel the same way? Is she pushing you to get rid of the competition? There are plenty of tourists and local traffic to support both businesses. There's no reason we can't coexist."

His hesitation covered up his regroup. Finally, he snorted. "I don't know why I'm even talking to you. I should be proposing this to Wesley." A mean glint shone in his eye. "Oh yeah. I can't. He's in jail for murder."

Reveling that I had a tiny advantage over him, I retorted, "Old news, Reginald. Wesley's out and not likely to return to jail."

"I don't care." Shaking a fist, Reginald blew out his fury. "I want this place gone, and I'll do whatever it takes to make it so. I have influence in this town. I can hold up permits, delay deliveries. You don't know trouble until you've messed with me."

"Reggie-baby, if this place goes under, it won't be because of you." This time, I folded my arms across my chest. "Don't let the door hit you on your way out."

I wondered if he had a similar conversation with Melody. I was sure her response, although nicer, would've been the same as mine, even considering the ferocity of his threats.

Reginald moved up on my suspect list from a tie with Vernelle to number one.

Chapter Thirty-Two

T he door slammed after Reginald, and I dropped onto a work stool. Breathing deeply, I calmed myself in minutes. Determined more than ever to keep Layers open, I began to sketch out a work schedule for Libby and myself.

A text tone pulled my attention from the work. It was Jake. *Can we meet?*

I answered that I could meet him at the bakery. He said he'd be there in ten minutes.

When he arrived, Jake ignored the *Closed* sign and walked in the back door. He held a cardboard cup of coffee. I'd had a cup this morning at home, but nothing since. Firing up the coffee maker here at the bakery was a laborious job and way too much trouble for one cup.

"Ohhhh, coffee," I cooed as I took the hot cup. "I could kiss you."

Jake lifted his eyebrows. "I didn't think Sensible Sarah said things she didn't mean."

"Uh," I scrambled to find the right words. "I only meant I was happy to see the coffee... and you, of course." I felt my cheeks warming. What was wrong with me? Facing him, I snapped off the plastic lid and sloshed steaming hot coffee on my fingers.

I yelped as I put the cup down on the worktable. Jake took my elbow and steered me over to the huge aluminum sink. Holding the scalded hand, he turned the cold water tap on and adjusted the stream to a little more than a trickle. He gently held my fingers, splaying them out to get maximum cooling with the least amount of water pressure.

I found myself pressing against his shoulder. I couldn't think of a reason other than it felt good. Solid and sturdy, but not immovable. His masculine scent was from soap and not cologne. Oh my. I straightened and pulled away as the pain subsided. "That's enough." Inspecting my fingers, I said, "I don't think this will even blister, thanks to your quick intervention."

He towered over me. I'm five foot ten, and I estimated his height at six three. I felt his breath on my hair. "It was nothing." He let go of my hand and traced the contour of my cheek with a finger.

No. We weren't going there. I'd finally severed my ties with Blaine, legally and emotionally. I wasn't ready for a new relationship, even though Jake was remarkably interesting. He held me at arm's length and looked at me. I felt like no one else had seen me like he did. His brown eyes delved into my soul. He knew me. He saw more than the 'Sensible Sarah' that everyone else knew.

"Ahem," I cleared my throat. It felt like a metaphor for clearing my brain. "So, why did you want to see me, Jake?"

He took a deep breath, clearing his own mind. "I went to see Vernelle Kearney last night. Wes's story is correct. She lied to us."

"We knew she was lying then." I waggled my fingers to keep the circulation going. "I'm glad she 'fessed up to you. Is she going to tell the truth when Kelly questions her? What about Wesley? Is he going to go to the sheriff's office and set his alibi?"

"She says she'll tell the truth. There's no point in lying now."

"She lied once. How do we know this is the truth?"

He smiled. "Because we want it to be true."

"We can't bank on that."

"I know. I'd hoped we could tie this up in a neat bow and hand it over to the Inyo district attorney seeing how Dorsey messed it up. But now..."

"And Wesley..."

Jake ran his fingers through his hair. "Wesley's another matter. He says he doesn't want to drag Vernelle Kearney through the court of public opinion."

"I'll talk to him if necessary. He's a fool to protect her when it could mean going to prison. It would be great if Vernelle would volunteer this info to the sheriff's office."

Jake shook his head. "I wouldn't count on that."

Chapter Thirty-Three

L ater that afternoon, Libby's motor scooter rumbled to a screeching stop in the back of Layers. Looking forward to seeing her, I met her at the door. It was easy to see why Melody took the time to invest in this young woman. She was clever and articulate, smart as they come and mature for her years. But she was also vulnerable. I got the feeling she held onto a great deal of pain. I'm sure she'd suffered over the loss of her mother, as all of us would. But the stigma of the rumors surrounding her death had a dear cost too. Suicide is never easy to understand. But how much worse it must be to believe your mother was a thief? Even living so distant, nine years ago, I heard about the embezzled funds from the medical equipment business where both her parents worked. They were our neighbors. Libby had been the real victim.

We'd arranged for her to stop by to go over the work schedule and a dozen other matters that needed to be resolved before Tuesday. Graduation was Monday night, and we'd decided we would open early Tuesday morning.

I warned her that she might miss grad parties that night, but she was adamant she wanted to get Layers up and running.

"I want to go over the recipes you're going to use. We need to order supplies and make signs. You'll have to tell your friend to update the website too."

Libby pulled out a binder with ragged edges of paper sticking out of the pages. Not tidy like Melody usually was. Yet, in my mind's eye, I saw Melody enthusiastically sticking recipe cards in the loose-leaf folder.

"Ooohhh, look at this one—blackberry pie." Libby touched the stained recipe card. "This reminds me of my mother's pies." She sat up, her eyes distant on a treasured memory from long ago. "We used to take a whole morning and pick berries before it got too hot. We'd come home with stickers in our fingers and purple tongues." She laughed. The sound resonated through the room. "I've definitely got to make this when berries are in season." She scanned the recipe with her phone.

Flipping through the pages, I found card after card of family favorites: chocolate crinkle cookies, my mom's cheesecake, strawberry, and rhubarb pie. We selected a half dozen pastries and desserts that Libby would bake regularly and several seasonal choices.

I closed Melody's binder and glanced at Libby. With her chin in a hand propped on the worktable, her eyes held a pensive quality. Her mother died nine years ago. She was still mourning. Wondering what Pandora's box I was opening, I felt like she wanted me to reach out. "You miss your mother."

"Uh hmm."

I held my silence. It was her choice if she wanted to talk or not. After a minute, she straightened. With a hand on the berry pie recipe, her eyes drilled into me. "I miss her, for sure. But I don't miss the arguments, though."

Every family had disagreements, but this didn't seem to be the time to minimize her recollection.

She blew out a deep sigh. "They fought that night, you know. The night she died." Libby's eyes sought out mine. "I'll never believe she killed herself. I mean, falling down the stairs wasn't the way anyone would pick, is it?"

"Your father must've been beside himself."

"It's a funny thing. He didn't mourn her. It was almost like he was relieved she was out of the way."

"Libby, people grieve in different ways. I'm sure he didn't..."

She slapped her hand on the worktable, startling me. "No. You don't get it. They hated each other by the time she died." Dormant grief held in too long lined her young face. "She blamed him for taking the money. I heard her yelling at him to turn himself in. After she died, he told the police that she was the one who'd embezzled from their boss. He let her take the blame, and she couldn't even defend herself."

Speechless at Libby's admission, I watched tears roll down Libby's cheeks. "Nobody believed me when I told them she didn't do it." She wiped at her eyes with a fist. "That's why I hate my father. I have since the day my mother died. And when I started working with Melody, he got jealous. Kept asking me questions about her like, 'What do you talk to her about? Did you say anything about me?' He's a narcissistic fool. Like he's all that." Translation to my millennial vocabulary, "Like he's something great."

An idea took bloom in my brain. What if Libby was right—Grant killed his wife. What if Grant quizzed Libby to find out what Melody knew about Norrie Armstrong's death? No one had listened to nine-year-old Libby's claims, and today, she herself doubted the reality of what she'd overheard. Apparently, her father had discounted Libby's observations as the product of his daughter's overactive imagination. Could Grant suppose Melody had listened to Libby's ravings and learned the truth about that night? Would he have come down to her house and, finding her in the dirt, finish Melody off?

Libby paled and sat staring at the door to the front counter area. I couldn't tell if she was reviewing everything she'd just said or off in la-la-land. Her father had never been on my radar as a suspect, but now it seemed reasonable. "Sarah," she said, her voice low as she faced me. "What if my dad thought Melody found out he'd killed Mom? What if he offed her?" She crumpled to the table, sobbing and burying her face in her arms. Muffled, she said, "It would be my fault. I told Melody what I heard."

I shook her, grabbed her shoulders, and made her look at me. "Listen to me. None of this is your fault. If your father did what you think, it's all on him. Not you."

She reached for me and shrank into my arms, sobbing like a five-year-old whose puppy had died. I stroked her back like a mother would and silently vowed to find the truth.

She had to know if she would ever have any peace.

Chapter Thirty-Four

I kept Libby with me at Layers knowing that going home would be the worst thing for her. I walked to a café a block north on Main Street and ordered sandwiches for lunch to go. Back at Layers, Libby struggled to compose herself as she ate.

We were picking up our trash from lunch when Jake texted asking me to call him.

"Hey, you." he said with a smile in his voice.

"Hey yourself."

"Kelly and I want to round up interested parties for questions. Is Layers still a good place?"

"Sure. When do you want to do this?"

"This afternoon, if that fits into your schedule."

"I don't have one yet, so this afternoon is fine. How about three o'clock? There are only two rooms that are usable for interviews, the counter in front and the kitchen. There's a tiny office upstairs, more like a cubby, where Libby and I can do our paperwork."

"That'll work great."

I scooped our account books and took them upstairs.

Libby followed with the recipes; her shoulders slumped. Sure that she was worried about her future after graduation in two days, I touched her arm as she slid the binder onto a desk. I pointed to a stool, and she settled on it without saying anything. "I can see you're still upset. Is it because of your impending graduation?"

She waved the thought away. "It's something I have to sort out before I talk to anyone. I'm just thinking."

"Do you need to be alone?"

Libby shrugged, which I took as a yes. "I'll be back in a little while. Use this room as long as you like." I grabbed the books from the desk and opened the door.

Downstairs, the back door opened. I heard Kelly greet Vernelle Kearney. I hoped Vernelle would make an official amendment to her statement from Thursday. The fact that she was in the same room as Deputy Kelly McSorley encouraged me to think she would recant her story about being home alone. I especially didn't want my presence to influence or scare off any impending confessions. Okay, not a confession of guilt, but at least an explanation. So I sat at the top of the stairs, putting the books down without noise. Settling in with nothing else to do, I listened to the conversation below. I heard Arco's nail clicking on the concrete floor and a sharp command. Arco must've sat because I didn't hear him walking around anymore.

Kelly didn't bother introducing Vernelle to Jake. The deputy ushered her to the front room. Minutes later, there was another knock at the back door. Reginald Bateau's voice boomed in greeting. He'd not met Jake formally yet and had no idea he was a policeman. I was curious to see how Reginald related to Jake. I heard stools being dragged across the floor, and I imagined them sitting at the worktable. From my vantage point, I saw only Reginald.

Jake kept his voice low and relaxed. He introduced himself as a policeman from Petaluma, California. He spoke a bit louder when he said, "I'm here helping Deputy McSorley with statements about the Melody Charters murder."

Reginald's face flushed. He jumped up and knocked over his stool. "You cops got me here under false pretenses. When he called to make this appointment, McSorley said he wanted my input. That doesn't equate to a statement. This isn't legal."

Jake's calm tone soothed Reginald's ruffled feathers. While I couldn't hear all that Jake said, Reginald picked up his stool and sat back down.

Leaving the books on the floor, I sidled down one step until I could see Jake. He had a notebook, like the ones the cops on TV use. His pen was poised as he listened to Reginald's answer.

"What make of car do you drive, Mr. Bateau?"

"A red SUV, a Ford Explorer."

"Deputy McSorley tells me that you live up on Bear Creek Drive. That's the north part of town, right?"

"Yes, it's behind the Rite Aid." At Jake's silence, he added, "Across from the casino right at the edge of town."

Jake nodded as if the knowledge of the world had opened up to him. "Do you know anyone who lives in Wilkerson?"

"Sir," Reginald's chest puffed out with indignation. "I know many, many people. I don't know where they all live. Maybe some of my employees live down there. How am I supposed to know?"

"Is there a reason you would be down there on Wednesday night?"

"Wednesday, Wednesday." Reginald tapped his chin as if it would help him remember. "I don't recall." He pulled out his phone and scrolled to the calendar. "Nope. Nothing for Wednesday night." He slipped the phone back into his shirt pocket.

With an understanding nod, Jake scratched in his notebook.

Reginald leaned forward, his anxiety finally showing. "What are you putting down there? I didn't say anything of consequence. What is this?"

I heard the faint chime of the front door opening. Kelly must have shown Vernelle out that way. I hoped he got the truth this time.

"I'm just recording your answers, Mister Bateau. It's all very innocuous, just to jog my memory if I'm asked. Besides, you don't have anything to hide. Do you, Mister Bateau?"

Reginald stood again, his face reddening. His blood pressure must have been through the roof. "Of course, I don't have anything to hide. What are you insinuating?"

Suddenly I felt Libby next to me. I hadn't heard her approach and wondered how much she'd heard.

"Jake, ask him what kind of car his wife drives."

Jake and Reginald looked up in surprise. Reginald hadn't expected anyone to be in the same room. He dropped to his stool. I had a feeling that Jake knew I was there but was surprised at Libby's comment.

Reginald shouted, "Shut up, you little twit."

Jake eyed Reginald. "What kind of car does your wife drive, Reginald?"

"A 2020 Hyundai Sonata."

"A coupe or sedan?"

"It's a two-door, if you must know."

"What color is it, Mister Bateau?"

Reginald sighed as if the tedium was getting to him. "White. It's white."

Jake leaned toward Reginald. "Mister Bateau, I'm going to ask you again. Please be sure of your answer, as lying to the police is against the law. Are you sure you weren't in Wilkerson on Wednesday night?"

Reginald clenched his fists like hammers. "You're trying to railroad me, aren't you? You must already know I was there. Why else would you threaten me?"

"That was no threat, Mister Bateau." Jake sat back. "That was a promise. You were in Wilkerson on Wednesday night. That has been established. Now, tell me the truth. What were you doing there?"

Reginald dropped his head in his hands as if the gesture would make Jake and his troubles go away. His hands, then his shoulders, began to shake, then his legs and feet. I was afraid he was having a seizure.

Suddenly he burst from the chair. "You... you... you idiots." He glanced at Jake then to Kelly, who'd just come into the room, then up the stairs to Libby and me. "You're always trying to get me in trouble. Just like school, you're bullying me for no good reason."

Jake stood, issuing a sharp command to hold Arco in position. Wary, Jake squared off with Reginald. It was easy to see there wasn't a gun or knife in Reginald's khakis or polo shirt. Yet he rose, full of fury and power, as if he had an atom bomb in his pocket. Kelly edged along the room very slowly, trying not to catch Reginald's attention.

Reginald swiveled around to Libby and me, shouting. "Get down here!"

"No!" Libby shouted, echoing my thoughts. Why would we come down? Not a chance.

"You… you… you don't know how much trouble you could be in if you don't pay attention to me."

Kelly froze ten feet away from the threat. Jake pushed the issue. "Why? What kind of trouble?"

Arco growled from deep within his chest. Reginald didn't know about Arco. Maybe he'd get a close-up chance soon.

Chapter Thirty-Five

"**B**etter than a gun or knives." Reginald eyed all of us, one at a time. "Better. You'll be sorry."

"Okay, Reginald. Let's just take it down a notch." Jake's soothing voice didn't placate Reginald. "What do you want? You want this all to go away? Well, it won't now. You've made everything much worse for yourself." Jake told Arco to stay. The dog must have responded to the tension in the room and stood up. I don't know what language it was, but it wasn't important. The tone of his master's voice made me pay attention.

"How much worse can it get?" Reginald's whine cut through Kelly's hesitation. He moved toward him again, very slowly.

Jake had caught Kelly's movement earlier and spoke up to keep Reginald's attention on him instead of the deputy. "Do you have a gun or any other weapon, Reginald?"

Reginald spat, "Gun? I don't need anything so pitiful. You fools will never know what hit you."

Jake repeated, "What is it that you want?"

Reginald spread his hands out to encompass the room. "This. I want this to go away."

"What?" I couldn't help myself. The idea that he'd hold us hostage so Layers would close permanently was absurd.

Reginald whipped his head around toward me. "I hate what this has done to me and my family."

Kelly was close. As long as Reginald focused on me, he wouldn't see Kelly or Jake. "What has Layers done to your family, Reginald?"

"My mother," he began with disgust. "She's relentless. She won't give up until I get rid of this place. She sees it as a threat to our business. She pushes and pushes me. She's threatening to give the bakery to her nephew. I'm getting an ulcer from it."

The back door flew open and slammed against the wall. A man's familiar voice shouted, "What's going on here?"

Reginald's head turned, as did almost everyone else in the room.

Not the lawmen. Kelly pounced on Reginald from behind like a fat cat on a rat. The two struggled on the floor while Jake wrestled Reginald's wrists for handcuffing. Arco's fur stood up along his spine. He barked furiously but again was overruled by his master. He quieted but remained standing, shaking with anticipation.

Finally, Reginald gave in. His shoulders shook with sobs. He had to realize it was over with two giant cops on top of him. Bernal, the PI who'd been following me, stood in the doorway, eyes hooded as he took in the scene.

Jake glanced at him with a nod, then turned Reginald

over. He pulled him up to a seated position, handcuffs secured his wrists behind him. "Do you have any weapons? This time, you answer with the truth."

Reginald hung his head and wobbled. He was having trouble balancing himself between the handcuffs and weeping. He shook his head. "No."

Jake grabbed a handful of polo shirt, forcing Reginald to look at him. "Gas? Explosives?"

I shuddered, considering the world Jake lived in. I hadn't thought of those weapons. Thank God he was here. And Bernal. What was *he* doing here?

"No, no." Reginald looked at Jake with terror in his eyes. "I'd never do anything like that."

Libby shouted at him, spitting in her fury. "Right. And you'd never kill anyone either. Would you?"

"I swear. I didn't know she was hurt."

Libby wasn't having any of it. "You slimy, deceitful..."

Jake saw the danger of their case going down the drain. "Deputy, Mirandize this dirtbag, quick."

I knew spontaneous confessions could endanger the most solid cases. I didn't know how strong Kelly's case would be, but this could put it at risk. Kelly leaned in to yell the Miranda admonishment above Reginald's crying admission. "Do you understand these rights?"

Reginald hiccuped. "I, uh... yes, I understand. But I didn't plan it. She just... she just wouldn't listen. I guess I got a little loud because she kept backing up. She tripped over a rock and fell. That's it. That's all that happened. She must've hit her head. I don't know..."

"You didn't see if she needed help," Libby yelled. I held her back on the stairs. She was ready to take Reginald on. "You could've saved her. She didn't have to die."

"I know... I know..."

Kelly and Jake picked up a rumpled, slobbering Reginald and marched him out the back door. It was the last we would see of him for some time.

Chapter Thirty-Six

Bernal stood by until Reginald was safely in Kelly's patrol car on his way to jail. Jake summoned Arco and put him in a down position beside him. Then Jake invited the PI inside while Libby and I came downstairs. Libby took a seat on a stool, wide-eyed.

"Sarah, this is Ruben Bernal. He's the guy who's been following you." Jake stepped beside me. I wasn't sure if he thought he was being protective, which I didn't need. Still, it felt good to have him there.

"Turns out it was a good thing, right?" I smiled at Bernal, feeling like he was on my side, not Blaine's.

"Yes." His bald head bobbed in agreement. "I saw what looked like a hostage situation unfolding inside. I decided that since he didn't have a gun or knife, I'd take a chance to distract him. Your friend, here," he pointed to Jake, "he pays attention. He saw me through the window and gave me the okey-doke."

"All this through a window." I was amazed at the wordless forms of communication cops employed. They probably had secret handshakes too. "But I assumed

Blaine's contract with you ended. No offense, but why are you still around?"

"None taken." He squinted as if debating how much to tell me. "You're ex, he's a..." Bernal grimaced. "He's a *cabron*."

Libby laughed and slapped a hand on her thigh. While delighted that she'd snapped out of her funk, I wondered how she knew enough about Blaine to agree with Bernal's appraisal.

I nodded. He captured Blaine's character without any input from me.

"This was a simple 'follow and find dirt' job. Even though you are divorced, he thought if he had something on you, he could force you back with him."

I sighed. "It's not because he loves me. He needs a meal ticket. If he's pushing for me to come back, he needs money yesterday. He doesn't have time to court and marry a new wife." Bernal's take on the assignment saddened me. I'd thought Blaine was selfish and single-minded, but to go to this length made me feel sorry for him. Not in a good way. "Did he pay you yet? Never mind. It's none of my business..."

"We're good." Bernal's lips thinned with disgust. "My partner's handling the invoicing."

I suspected his partner would have his hands full collecting from Blaine. I hadn't realized how badly my ex had managed his finances until the financial declaration during the divorce proceedings. After settling his debts, I'd come out with barely enough to put down for my first and last month's rent on an apartment. The Camry was paid off, thank goodness. I was well and truly starting over. "So, back to my earlier question. Why are you still here?"

Bernal rubbed a hand over his bald head in thought.

"Like I told you the other night, I'm a retired cop. I can feel when something's not right. It didn't take long for me to figure you out." He surprised me with the kindest smile, at odds with the tough, macho exterior he presented. "You're a nice lady. You go to church and help your neighbors." He nodded toward Libby. "The longer I watched, the more wrong I knew he was about you. Then, I got a feeling that I wasn't alone. I was watching you, and so was someone else. It gave me the creeps, you know?"

"That's not good, Bernal." Jake's jaw tensed. "Did you get a look at him?"

"No. I never saw anyone. It's just a feeling, like seeing a shadow where there shouldn't be one."

We stood in silence for a moment, each deep in thought about what this could mean. Then, Bernal shrugged. "I stayed... well, I waited to find the right time to tell you." He looked to Jake and said with a toothy smile, "I wanted him to know too."

Jake curled a protective arm around my shoulders. I thought it overly dramatic, but it felt good, so I didn't move away. "And Arco too. He's a real guardian angel," I said as I leaned down to stroke his head. "He seems more relaxed now that Reginald is gone."

Both men nodded. "Animals have a sense about people, but dogs especially." Jake said.

"Well, now that the killer is in jail, I think we can all relax." Libby said.

Jake put his hand up. "Not so fast. Reginald confessed, but there are questions that need to be answered."

"That'll be for the Inyo County sheriff to figure out." Bernal eyed him. "You work for a different agency, if I'm correct. Not even in this county."

"Petaluma Police up in Sonoma County, north of San Francisco."

Bernal nodded.

I wondered how much longer Jake would be able to stay. I knew he'd taken family leave from the department, but when would he return? He'd mentioned he had a lieutenant's exam coming up.

Wondering at the unhappiness creeping inside, I realized Jake would be returning to his hometown—soon.

Chapter Thirty-Seven

Jake and I met Kelly at the substation after dinner at a Murray family-favorite Mexican restaurant. Bernal had begged off at our offer of dinner and left for the long drive back to Los Angeles. Libby went home. She'd been reluctant but gave in after Grant texted that he would be out of town for business for the next two days. Arco, as always, was by Jake's side.

On the off chance that Kelly hadn't had time to eat after booking Reginald, I brought him a takeout plate of beef tacos, chicken enchiladas, beans, and rice. The Kelly I knew in high school was a big eater. Judging by the extra holes on his duty belt, that hadn't changed. Arco sat at Jake's command but watched every move Kelly made. His pitiful eyes made me laugh.

"Don't you ever feed your dog?"

"He looks pathetic, doesn't he? It's a ruse. He gets plenty to eat, but the vet put him on a diet right before we left, so he feels he's missing out."

We laughed again as Arco watched Kelly scoop the beans and rice together and shoveled them into his mouth. He talked between mouthfuls. "Reginald is booked for manslaughter. The district attorney can upgrade the charge to murder if he wants."

Jake asked, "What did he say in the interview?"

Kelly mopped up the last of the beans with a flour tortilla. Wiping his hands and face, he sat back in his chair, thinking about his answer. "Just like he said before. He's consistent that he followed Melody home. She was not too far from the house looking for your dog. He hollered at her, and she started to walk in. He walked out to meet her. He said he was upset, yelling. He'd just gotten into a beef with his mother, who's threatening to take the bakery away from him. Anyway, he says she got scared and started backing up. She tripped over a rock, fell, and hit her head on another rock. She laid there, not moving. He said he was going to check on her, but he thought about how it would look to everyone. That he'd pushed his competition to her death. Says he didn't know if she was breathing or not. He just hot-footed it out of there."

"He didn't see Arco?"

"Nope."

"He didn't see or hear anyone else out there? I mean, I went off looking for Arco in the opposite direction. If he'd called out, I could've come to help." Jake shook his head.

"Nope. At least he's in custody which is where he needs to be."

"Are you sure?" Jake's statement about more questions hung in my mind.

Jake had the same thought and said, "Reginald said she fell backward onto a rock. I thought the coroner's report said..."

"I know, I know." Kelly mopped red sauce from his fingers. "That's been bugging me too."

He wheeled the chair from the table where his meal was to the computer monitor. He pulled out the mouse, scrolled, and tapped until he found the correct document. He scanned it until he came to Melody's cause of death. "Blah, blah, blah. Here we are. 'Blunt trauma of head with skull fracture and brain injury. Manner of death is homicide'."

"Is there any indication of more than one injury site?" Jake looked over his shoulder. "There, there." Jake pointed. "'The appearance of wood fiber in the wound indicates interference with a wooden object, possibly a stick or a tree branch'."

Kelly sat back, wide-eyed. "Does this mean there were two killers?" A sweat broke out on his forehead. "Two killers? A person can't be killed twice. Can they?"

His face grim, Jake said, "Yes. You have to look at intent and means. If two people had a hand in killing Melody Charters, that means there's still a killer out there."

"No way." Kelly whispered, wiping his brow. We sat in stunned silence.

I broke the stillness. "What now?"

Jake twirled Kelly around in the chair to face him. "You need to go to the DA. You can't trust your boss with this."

"But…" Kelly couldn't find the words to protest.

Chapter Thirty-Eight

The evening was cooling nicely for early June, from a daytime temperature of ninety degrees to an expected low in the mid-fifties. I hadn't brought a sweater with me, and I shivered as Jake and I left the substation. Jake put an arm around my shoulders in the absence of a jacket. I savored his smell and the comfort his embrace gave me for a moment. Then I broke away. "Do you think Kelly's going to the DA?" We ambled toward my car in the parking lot.

"No idea." Jake shook his head. "He knows what he should do. I can't force him, so I have to walk away from it."

"I understand the jurisdictional issue, but what's the right thing to do here?"

In the streetlights, his eyes held a faraway look. "I've done what I can do."

"What about Wesley?"

Jake groaned. "That's something else. As of this morning, his plan was to work with Anna and Tom to put on the memorial service for Melody next week. Friday, I think."

"You think?" I patted his chest. "How could you be confused about such an important event?"

With a rueful smile, he said, "He's changed his mind more times than I can count. First, because of the investigation, Melody's body hasn't been released for burial. Then, Anna and Tom had made arrangements for the service. I think he's going with their plans. He can't preside over it himself, so he has to count on colleagues nearby. With the scandal over his arrest, he's not had much cooperation. Poor guy. He loses his wife, gets arrested for killing her, then has this much trouble burying her."

"My heart goes out to him. They were so much in love. They so wanted to start a family." We stopped at my Camry. "What's he going to do? Will the elders let him continue as pastor?"

"He's not sure. He hopes so, but they won't decide until next week sometime."

"What about you?" I stopped and stared into his lovely brown eyes. "When do you go home?"

The question seemed to jerk him into a reality he hadn't wanted to face just yet. He looked away. "I have a lieutenant's test on Monday. If I leave tomorrow, I'll have time to study."

"Will you be back for Melody's service?"

He smiled a soft, gentle smile that was so easy to get lost in. More than his usual half smile. "I wouldn't miss it."

"We'll stay in touch, right?" That was as much as I could commit. I really liked Jake. My affection and respect grew for him every time I was around him. But with Blaine still in my recent past, I wanted to take it slow.

"You bet." He reached up and touched my cheek, tracing my jawline. My pulse quickened, and I found myself short of breath.

"I'll see you soon, then." I turned and opened the door of my car. I got in feeling like I was hurrying away from... what? I missed him already.

I rolled my window down at his gesture. "Watch your back, Sarah. You've been snooping around this investigation. Somebody might think you know something that could put him—or her—in jail."

I gave him a thumbs-up sign and drove off.

Chapter Thirty-Nine

Libby ran into the kitchen, pacing, her face twisted with anger. "I can't believe it. Reginald Bateau has been released from jail."

It was almost noon, and I'd just finished the laundry order. I sent the order to the service and a copy to my laptop file. "What? Are you kidding?"

She stopped and stared at me solemnly. "I'd never joke about something like this, Sarah."

In the week since Reginald's arrest, we'd had a flurry of activity. Libby graduated on Monday night. I was there to celebrate with her. I got a giant smile and hug for my efforts. It was worth it. Because she had to get up so early the next morning, Libby chose not to party with her classmates. She and I shared a frozen yogurt in town, then went home. Grant was nowhere to be seen. I got a shrug when I asked when he would return from his business trip. I didn't want to press her. She had enough on her mind.

Tuesday was Layers' reopening day. We'd anticipated

a slow first day but were surprised at the local turnout. Some tourist traffic appeared as it was the beginning of summer, but the locals really pushed our sales over the top. We only opened for four hours, from six-thirty to ten-thirty. Until we became more established, we'd keep that schedule.

Melody's memorial service had been moved out another week. I was glad for Wesley when he called to tell me he'd found someone to perform the service. He also mentioned Jake would be returning. But I knew that. Jake and I had stayed in touch, mostly by text, but he called nearly every evening. I pictured him sitting in his patrol SUV on his break, dodging Arco's slobbers.

The level of trust between us grew. We talked about his family and how his father had divorced his mother and married Wesley's. They hadn't had an amicable relationship until they were adults. Jake, at thirty-six, was senior by seven years to Wesley. Jake and Wesley had fallen into a wonderfully comfortable big brother/little brother relationship. Wesley even got Jake to go back to church.

But now I looked at Libby's furious bearing. "I don't get it. I just don't understand. A guy confesses to killing Melody, gets arrested, and somebody sets him free from jail."

"Hard to believe..."

"No, it's outrageous. We should start a petition to have him slapped back into prison."

I resisted patting her hand when I said, "That's not how it works."

"How does it work?"

I explained the arrest process and added that my experience was in Los Angeles. Although it was generally similar, each county has their own procedures and peculiarities. In Inyo County's case, it could be that the district attorney decided a lesser charge was appropriate, enabling Reginald to be eligible for bail, supervised release, or release on his own recognizance. I thought the former was more probable. "We aren't allowed to see all the evidence because it's not public information. Making a judgment without all the facts is unwise, no matter how we feel about him. You never know if someone stepped up to clarify Reginald's confession. Maybe the second killer presented himself." Unlikely, but possible.

"It's still bu…"

"Stop." I put my hand up, just like I remember Melody doing at camp when we were kids. "Cussing is a sign of a weak vocabulary."

"Okay, okay. I get it." She huffed indignantly and plopped down on a stool. "I get why everyone teases you as Sensible Sarah." She relaxed as she said, "You always have a logical perspective on things. I'm more emotional, so I depend on you. Melody was the same way. Maybe a little different, but it's easy to see that you two are related and spent your childhood together."

The loss of my cousin clutched my heart in a surprise grip. To change the subject, I asked, "What's the info on the new pastry shop in town? You hear anything?"

"Oh!" She jumped up, anxious to share her news. "Oh yeah, I forgot to tell you. Word from the hardware store, Inyo Transit, and the newspaper is that we're the place to go on the way to work."

Delighted with this update, I hugged her. She held on a little longer than I did.

"I'm sorry. That was awkward. I'm just starting to feel like we're friends. More than neighbors or boss and employee."

Putting my hand on hers finally seemed appropriate. "I agree, Libby. We're friends."

We hugged again, and I wondered how much of her rumor had been driven by Reginald's release. No one wanted to hang out with a murderer, much less eat his donuts or drink his coffee. Reginald was being avoided.

Chapter Forty

Six o'clock came early every morning. Libby baked from four o'clock until opening, until orders were filled and items were sold. After ten days, we were consistently making money. The end of my second week was coming to a close when I heard from the Inyo County Court. They offered me a full-time job in Bishop. This was the answer to my earlier prayers, although soon after I took over Layers, I stopped praying. I hoped my request would be answered, but a little later. I wanted to get this bakery off the ground. I wanted to make a success of Melody's dream. I also wanted to help Libby become the person she could be. There was so much potential in that girl that sometimes I found it difficult not to hug her. And I knew Bishop had more Libbys waiting for the help Layers could provide—a skill set that would be welcome in the food service and hospitality industries. Learning to show up on time, to do what you're asked to do efficiently, and show initiative during downtime would serve in any job. But the most cogent lesson would be what to do with the trust they'd have when they walked through the back door.

Now the county offered something that would alter *my* future. I wasn't sure it was what I wanted now—or needed. I thought it over, talked with Jake, Mom, and Dad, and finally decided I'd pass on this round. The human resources person told me there were several retirements looming late this year, so I wasn't shutting the door.

With luck, I'd get Layers running well enough to hire someone to manage the business and the nonprofit side, then I'd be free to go back to work, even buy a home. I truly did love my job. But I loved Layers and Libby too.

All of these things passed through my head in a flash of reminiscence as I doled out coffees and pastries at the curb. Libby had found a Starbucks-trained barista and hired her on the spot. My baker saw how far I stretched every morning making designer coffees (well, we offered them on our website), dashing out to the curb to deliver goods, and boxing up donuts. I could've kissed Libby for her resourcefulness. The barista alone was worth every penny of her salary. She also kept her tips.

The next order for seven o'clock was a box of mixed donuts and four coffees to the green Chevy pickup parked in front of the shop. Balancing the box and the cardboard coffee holder at the passenger door, I handed them off and pocketed a nice five-dollar bill for the tip jar. The cheery, "Have a lovely day." brought a smile to my face. Savoring the brisk Bishop morning, I turned to get back to work. My eye caught a white Ford pickup parked kitty-corner in a parking lot. The business to which the lot belonged was closed, as were the two other stores surrounding it. I looked at my watch. Just seven-fifteen. The earliest one of those businesses would open was nine.

I squinted against the morning sun and noticed the outline of a figure inside. He was watching me. I was sure of it.

I hurried inside and grabbed my phone. I texted Bernal. *Are you awake?*

His answer, *Sure, isn't everyone?* Smart-aleck.

Are you watching me?

No. This time I felt his concern. *Take a picture of the vehicle and send it to me.*

I stepped outside with my phone. The truck was gone.

He's gone.

Okay, don't worry, probably a turista infatuated with you.

Doubt it.

Tell Kelly. Give him a vehicle description. License plate? Can you ID the driver?

No on the plate. Not even sure it's a male.

Do what I tell you anyway. Macho so-and-so. But warmed at his caring.

Okay. Thanks.

We signed off.

It was after lunch when I got through to Kelly. I relayed the information, and it surprised me that he had a similar reaction to Bernal. I figured Kelly would think I was imagining things, but I felt satisfied that he took the incident seriously.

I had decided not to tell Libby because I didn't want to burden her with my troubles. Grant had come home, and she spent much of her time off dodging him. Their relationship seemed to be worsening. I also didn't tell Jake. He was eight hours away and couldn't do anything to help.

I didn't think much could be done anyway.

Chapter Forty-One

Melody's memorial service was unforgettable, to say the least. Held in Wesley's church almost two weeks after her death, every pew was occupied. The elders had welcomed him back, and all attended. Overflow mourners stood in the back and in the side aisles. We expected a crowd of people because Melody was a hometown girl, but the number of mourners astonished even Wesley. Libby had told us there were folks in town who still believed Wesley had something to do with Melody's death. If that was the case, they must have tallied in a single digit. Few, if any, were staying away. It made my heart swell at the depth of feeling the community held for my cousin.

Wesley's colleague had known Melody and his eulogy reflected her loving personality. In another tribute, my father spoke about Melody's growing up years and her determination to serve God, to do the right thing, and how she championed those less than fortunate. When he read off a list of her accomplishments within the community, I was blown away. There were many projects she had done but hadn't shared with me. Many tears were shed at the thought of the loss of this generous soul.

She'd done so much, so quietly.

At the reception, the room filled quickly. Many were family members, both close and distant relatives. Cameron Scherwin was there to lend an arm for Libby to lean on. I was pleased to see people with whom Melody and I had attended school from kindergarten to high school. We even welcomed some former summer campers. It felt as much a reunion for me as an event to honor Melody.

Jake had made an overnight trip for the service but had to be back to work the next day. We had little time together. He spent most of it with Wesley, as he should. At the reception, he told me that Kelly was unsuccessful at getting the district attorney to investigate the possibility of two people responsible for Melody's murder.

It wasn't long before the caterers ran out of food. I sent Libby to Layers to pack up anything that could be served. She returned with sourdough rolls, croissants, pastries, and muffins. I'm certain every mourner was sent home with their appetite satisfied. When I got back to the bakery afterward, my heart was full of the treasures from these wonderful people who Melody loved so much.

Libby had been up since four in the morning baking, and the emotional drain of the day had taken a toll. I planned to take her home, then return the trays to Layers. When I dropped her off, we both breathed a sigh of relief that Grant's white Ford pickup wasn't in the driveway.

I parked my Camry in the small lot behind the shop. Balancing the trays after struggling to wrestle keys from my purse, I noticed the door was unlocked. It was unlike Libby to leave the door open, but I couldn't fault her. She came to our rescue at the reception and, in her haste, had forgotten to lock the door. It was as simple as that.

I dropped my purse on a table and slid the aluminum trays into a sheet pan rack. Out-of-place pans caught my eye, as well as Springform pans scattered on the floor. We'd made a storage cubby under the stairs. To make it work, we'd moved an unused proofing oven to the office. Even though the oven was small, it was heavy enough that it took both Libby and me to haul it up the stairs. The office often held unusable equipment until we figured out what to do with it. This oven was awaiting repair from an out-of-town appliance repair service.

I bent over to pick them up. I heard an unfamiliar sound to this room. Something out of the ordinary alerted me. I backed up in time to feel the rush of air from the proofing oven hurtling to the floor—where I'd just been standing. It sat in a fissure almost six inches deep.

The heavy aluminum slamming to the floor knocked me off my feet. Dazed, I glimpsed a figure rushing down the stairs and out the door. On the floor, I laid against a leg of the worktable and took a deep breath. The first one in over a minute, but at least it wouldn't be my last.

Chapter Forty-Two

Kelly finished recording my answers and flipped his notebook closed. "Sarah, you'd better be careful." he mumbled, his round face dark with concern.

I cut across his warning. "I'm not doing anything threatening to anybody. I don't get it. It's not like the first week I got here when I was snooping around. I mean, Reginald is going to court next month. He's pleading guilty to manslaughter, for crying out loud."

Kelly's face was grim. "Did you forget there is probably another killer out there? He's the guy who did this." He pointed to the damaged oven sitting in the hole in the concrete floor.

"I'm not sure this was secured when we moved it upstairs. It could have been an accident."

Kelly's face twisted in a look of doubt. "Don't think so."

"But why? I'm no danger to anyone." I kicked at the chunks of concrete. "What is he afraid of?"

"Don't have a clue." Kelly's big shoulders squeezed in

a shrug. "But you better think about not spending much time alone. Keep someone with you."

"I can't do that. I open this place at six in the morning. Libby's busy with baking, and Emma, the barista, is always on the run."

"You'll be safe then. What about after?"

"I usually go for a walk."

"There. Don't go alone."

My phone vibrated in my pocket. Blaine. What could he want? A fleeting suspicion darted into my mind. I wondered if he was in the area. If nothing else, he'd be an excuse to conclude my uncomfortable conversation with Kelly. "Sorry, Kel. I've got to take this."

I walked to the front counter as I heard the back door slam after Kelly. "Blaine?"

"Sarah, glad you answered." He didn't need to know why. "I need your help."

"No, already, Blaine. I'm not loaning you any money." I didn't have any to loan, although Layers was doing well enough that I'd begun to pay Libby a salary in addition to Emma's part-time pay. If business activity continued through next month, I'd sort out a salary for myself. That is, after I paid into the nonprofit.

He tsked, "No, it's not that. It's Rusty. I need your help with him." His voice had lost the lovesick tone he'd tried on me last time. This was the real Blaine, the guy who really needed help. Not the manipulating joker who used me to obtain the finer things in life, like a home.

"What do you need?" I was long past answering Blaine with an automatic, 'Yes, I'll help.' Still, I pictured horrible dog illnesses and injuries.

"Rusty keeps running away. I've put him in doggie daycare, but it costs an arm and a leg. He even runs off from there, even though he loves it. I can't manage him anymore." Elated over where this was going, I managed to keep quiet until he finished talking. "Can you take him?"

"Yes." This was one question I'd answer an immediate yes to. "When can I get him? Will you bring him up here?"

"I can't. I've got to go out of town tomorrow for a job." I heard him suck a breath in between his teeth. "Can you come get him?"

"Tomorrow? Yes." I considered who would work the cash register tomorrow while I spent all day on the road fetching my dog. I'd call Anna. She'd offered her help before. "Where are you living? I need your address."

"I got an apartment in Burbank... It's all I could afford."

"Give me the address."

He did.

"Will you be there to let me in?"

His whine started up. "No, I leave for Mexico City on an early flight. I'll leave a key under the doormat."

"Okay. I'll be there before noon to pick him up. Gather all his toys, food, and bed for me, please." I'd hate to have to hunt all that up in his new house. On his best day, Blaine wasn't organized. He probably still had moving boxes in the living room.

Chapter Forty-Three

I left at seven o'clock after making sure Anna knew what to do. Emma and Libby were there if she needed help, but I was confident Anna could do the job. She was excited to be there, to be part of her daughter's bakery dream.

The drive to Burbank normally took four hours. The Camry was a comfortable car in which to travel these high desert highways. I took Highway 395 to Highway 14 south past Lancaster and Palmdale, outliers of the Los Angeles metro area. The 14 was also called the Antelope Valley Freeway, where it traversed the Angeles National Forest. Just before Antelope Valley Freeway dropped into the San Fernando Valley, it merged with Highway 5. I traveled the last fifteen miles, white-knuckled, to Blaine's address on East Providence in Burbank. I used to zip all over these highways with no thought. But having lived in Bishop for two months, the traffic and noise got to me.

I pulled up in front of Blaine's apartment building

before eleven. I'd made good time. I hoped to make it quick in Burbank and get home. The apartment was a step-down for Blaine. Squared boxes with no architectural style sat on pillars that covered carport parking. Still, it was clean, as was the neighborhood. A recent exterior painting was a plus. I was hopeful that he was learning to live within his means.

I found the key under the mat just as he said and let myself in to Rusty's welcoming bark. After bouncing with excitement, he let me hug him. His rust-colored coat was smooth and shiny. A shower of licks and anxious whines told me he was happy I was there. I didn't know how long it'd been since Blaine left, but I guessed it was time for Rusty to go outside. I looked around for dog stuff and found bowls on the floor where he'd been fed, presumably this morning.

Blaine hadn't packed any of Rusty's things. I searched for a grocery bag and went to what looked like a pantry. A ten-pound bag of kibble and a few cans of dog food. I'd have to buy some more at the feed store in Bishop. I tucked them into the bag. There were the dog cookies, Rusty's favorite, BaconBites. The food bowl went in the bag, but I left the water bowl out for Rusty. The bed would be in Blaine's bedroom. I'd get it last. But now he needed a break.

I found a harness and leash in the hall closet. I snapped them on and followed as Rusty took me for a short walk. Back in the apartment, I gave the kitchen and living room a cursory inspection for Rusty's toys. Rusty lapped up water from his bowl as I went into Blaine's bedroom.

It smelled of him, an expensive cologne—and of a woman's perfume. Oh my. I didn't want to be here. I felt like I was looking into a stranger's room, and it turned my stomach. I grabbed Rusty's pillow bed, snagged the bag with the water bowl, and ran to the front door. I locked the door and left the key where I found it.

Rusty and I headed home.

Chapter Forty-Four

W e arrived home around dinnertime. Wesley got there a half hour before and had been invited to stay for dinner. After wrestling with a young dog who'd been confined to a small car for four hours, I set him loose in the backyard. Then, I reached out to Wesley for a hug. It was awkward, full of worry about the other, each holding on too long.

Mom and Dad were happy to see Rusty. He'd always been welcome during Blaine and my visits home. They still missed Buster and talked about getting another dog. Now the discussion was postponed until I moved out.

After dinner, Wesley and I watched Rusty chase a ball in the backyard. "He's going to give you a run for your money."

"He's a young dog with lots of energy. Blaine said Rusty had started to run off and go roaming. I'll be taking him out for hikes for exercise and to poop him out. I'd like to go up to the Buttermilks, exploring."

Dad came out with a cup of coffee in his hand. After asking if we wanted anything to drink, he dropped into an Adirondack chair. Wesley sat beside him as I continued throwing the ball. The afternoon breeze had laid down, leaving the sagebrush scent permeating the air. It was heavenly.

Dad cleared his throat. This was a cue he'd used during my childhood. What followed would be important. I knew I'd better pay attention. "Sarah, you've been gone for ten years. It's easy to forget what is in the desert and mountains." His hand circled, indicating the Owens Valley, the Sierras, and the White Mountains. "This isn't Disneyland. It's not like LA, where there's more concrete than dirt."

"Dad, I remember..." I said, trying to reassure him.

The set jaw and stern eyes told me I'd better shut up and listen. "This area isn't for everyone. It's not like the movies. There are things here that will kill you dead faster than you can think about it."

Wesley nodded. "Rattlers, scorpions, and spiders—not all, but some are lethal. Bobcats, coyotes, and mountain lions roam these hills. Last year, a bear broke into one of the Aspendell cabins. Tore the whole place up."

Dad picked up the warning. "Then there's the weather. Extreme heat, wind that will sandblast a car, sudden rain squalls that could lead to flash flooding and mudslides. If you're hiking, a rockfall is something to watch out for. Be sure the terrain is stable before you walk on it."

Mom came out and laid out a tray of cookies. I reached for one hoping for a change of subject. Undeterred by snickerdoodles, Dad continued, "Speaking of terrain, watch where you walk. Volcanic vent holes opened by earthquakes aren't usually marked, so watch where you walk. Years ago, Mammoth Mountain lost three ski patrol members while they were trying to fence off the vent. I don't want to scare you from hiking, but I want you to be aware of what's out there."

"Dad, I learned all this in school." His face flushed. I hoped he didn't feel embarrassed. He only meant to keep me safe. "But you're right. I've been a flatlander for a long time. I needed this refresher."

Wesley snorted, "And that's only in the summer. Winter's a whole new ball game."

I stood, put my hand over my heart, and faced these three people who I loved so much. "Thank you for the warnings. I'll keep them in mind when we go."

Chapter Forty-Five

Jake texted he'd be coming down for a long weekend on Friday. I looked forward to seeing him but knew his focus was on his brother, as it should be. Wesley had been struggling with his own grief but was also determined to build his flock back to where it had been before Melody died. I'd hoped Jake would make me his secondary focus. We'd continued texting and talking almost daily but with no commitments from either. For now, his friendship was enough.

I didn't feel that I was all that good at relationships, anyway. Something I did or lacked made Blaine look elsewhere. Besides, long-distance relationships were hard enough without my recently added baggage.

The next few days were a blur of activity. Summer tourist traffic was in full gear, and locals were up before sunrise to beat the summer heat. Bishop's summer temperatures ranged from the mid-nineties during the day to the mid-forties at night. Ranching and agriculture were the nontourist industries in the Owens Valley. Mining had been big since the gold rush days beginning in 1849. Although scaled down, mining continued to the present day.

Rusty came to work with me every day. He slept on the landing just outside the office. He had a great view from there, he could see all the activity in the kitchen and seemed content. A walk to the canal three blocks away in the morning held him until we got off work. Then, I changed into tennis shoes, grabbed my backpack, and I drove the two of us up to the Buttermilks, a dramatic—and cooler—area, two thousand feet higher than town.

This was a small mountain range at an elevation of just over 6,000 feet on the western edge of the Owens Valley, in the Eastern Sierra foothills. One of its most famous attractions were the Buttermilk Boulders. Among rock climbers, the area is known for its large "highball" boulders. The boulders are glacial erratics, meaning they don't match the rest of the rock found in the area because they were carried from far away by glaciers. The area was active all year-round with hikers, campers, rock climbers, bicyclists, and horse and mule trail riders.

Only seven miles away from Layers, yet high enough in elevation that the air temperature was milder, I expected this to become our go-to place for summer walks. Rusty loved the wide-open dirt roads and often chased rabbits or squirrels or worse. I enjoyed getting out of the shop and breathing the dry desert air. I hoped walking would help me drop the few pounds I'd gained since working at the bakery. Libby was truly gifted and was now experimenting with her own recipes. The past week had brought us growing success. Libby swore it was local Boulangerie patrons shifting their loyalty to Layers because Reginald had confessed to harming one of their own. There was no accounting for the burgeoning tourist trade on Friday evenings and Sunday afternoons. We were just lucky, I guessed.

I didn't care. I was basking in the glow of moderate and steady gains. Libby and I were doing something right. Anna had enjoyed the work so much that she volunteered to come in twice a week to work for tips. Tomorrow, I planned to offer her a part-time position for an hourly wage. I was sure she'd accept. She and Tom had given me their blessing to continue working at Layers. Wesley had barely heard my request but, in the end, agreed.

Six days after Melody's memorial, on a warm afternoon, Rusty and I took off for the Buttermilk Road on foot. I'd not had any 'running off' problems with my dog as Blaine had complained about. Rusty needed generous exercise to curb his wanderings. The week's afternoon adventures filled the bill.

Yesterday we wandered off the road to a game trail that I hoped would lead to McGee Creek. It hadn't, but we found an abandoned mineshaft carved out of a hillside. Barricaded with rusted iron doors welded together, I was sure we wouldn't get inside. I was curious, but I had been raised with warnings about the dangers of abandoned mines in the desert. This one, however, seemed secure. A rusted ore car sitting on its side offered a comfortable seat to eat a snack. The scrub had diminished here due to the altitude, and the rocks were easy to navigate, so getting around wasn't tough. While eating, I threw sticks for Rusty, who ran after them with delight. After I finished my meal, I poured a bowl of water for him and waited for him to lap it up. I weighed walking for another half hour and decided both of us were up to it.

Up the trail, a hundred feet from the mine, a smaller

game trail led off. Wondering if it led anywhere interesting, I hiked on. A pile of day-old horse droppings meant we weren't as alone as it seemed. Rusty barked with excitement, bounding around the sagebrush. He rushed past me off the trail. I picked up a stick and threw it, hoping he'd catch up to it. He did and trotted off behind an enormous boulder. I worried when he didn't return.

When I rounded the boulder and saw him, I caught my breath. We had found an abandoned pack station. It was like seeing an Old West postcard come to life, this pack station was frozen in time. Sniffing the ground, Rusty inspected the corrals. Four huge roundups sat at the edge of a compound. Half a dozen outbuildings of varied sizes made it easy to pick out tack rooms, storage, bunk houses, and a business office. A long lean-to, connected to one of the larger corrals, bordered the back of the property. Aside from the disrepair and dust, packers could have left yesterday. The dry air in the Eastern Sierras desiccates wood instead of rotting it. There was no telling how long it had been abandoned. Windows and doors had been shuddered against weather. In early June, with beautiful blue skies overhead, it was clear no one would be back to open up anytime soon. "Look what we found, Rusty." Walking around the buildings was interesting, but there wasn't anything unusual to see. It was time to go.

Rusty continued sniffing the ground with the eager drive to know who'd been there before him. Dried-up piles of horse droppings were of particular interest. I hollered at him when he pawed at the ground. He'd rolled in a carcass before, and I didn't want to have to give him a bath tonight. His head shot up instantly, listening to me. When I told him to come, he took his time deciding, then broke into a run toward me.

I watched him bound around the brush and rocks, tongue lolling out of his mouth. What joy this animal brought me. This was one of the few moments I felt sorry for Blaine. He'd never appreciated Rusty for the wealth of happiness that he brought. The dog had only been a bargaining chip for him.

Following another narrow trail ten feet away, Rusty dove behind a man-sized boulder and was lost from view. A yelp and whine later, I knew he was in trouble. When I found him, his hind end had fallen through boards covering a hole. He clawed at the wood, trying to right himself. Praying this wasn't where an outhouse had been, I grabbed the nap of his neck. I reached down his back as far as I could, grabbed his coat, and pulled him up.

There was no tell-tale smell of a latrine. Relieved on several levels, I stroked my humiliated pooch. I checked him for injuries and found none. A minute later, he was trotting toward the corral.

Brushing the dust and stickers off, I stood and called him back to me. He'd better stay close to me. We just saw what kind of trouble he could get into exploring.

Soon, we piled back in the Camry and drove home with Rusty hanging his head out the passenger side window. Despite the near disaster, I predicted this walk would be a favorite.

We both slept soundly that night.

Chapter Forty-Six

Wednesday, three weeks after Melody's memorial, brought even bigger summer crowds. Anglers, campers, European travelers seeking the Old West experience, and rock climbers filled grocery stores, motels, and bakeries. Well, one bakery anyway—Layers. We'd expanded our hours and hired two more baker's assistants. Anna and I had the counter handled, with Emma pitching in as needed. I'd finally gotten the nonprofit paperwork approved and had met with the two high schools. Each school had identified two students interested in an apprenticeship, and the four were due to begin next week.

That was the first day I had an inkling of the trouble Boulangerie was in. At Layers that morning, Emma greeted me with news that Mildred Bateau had passed away the day before. Normally, such news brings me a moment of sadness. I understood grief and wished it on no one. Knowing it was a part of life made no difference. But Mildred Bateau was the matriarch of an Owens Valley baking dynasty. This was the end of an era.

Reginald hadn't yet gone to court, so he was still free, meddling with the daily operation of Boulangerie. Now with his mother out of the picture, I saw nothing but trouble for the bakery. And I wasn't happy about it. For years it had been a bastion of baked goods, attracting tourists from all over the world to enjoy French-inspired breads and pastries. I grew up with the Bateau cousins, and even though I never warmed to Reginald, I respected the business and the family.

In the kitchen at Layers, Libby glanced at her phone. She yipped at the screen and hollered to me in the doorway. "Did you hear?"

"Libby, I don't listen to gossip."

"Sarah, this isn't gossip. It's a fact—Boulangerie is in serious trouble." Finding it odd that she should come up with the same conclusion at the same moment, I hesitated.

It was all she needed. "They quit," she gushed. "All of 'em. Every single Boulangerie employee quit over Reginald's bullying."

"Oh, my Lord! What's he going to do?" I didn't realize I'd said it out loud until Libby replied.

She stuck her pierced nose in the air. "Don't know and don't care."

The shop door chimed, and I went back to the counter. I couldn't believe my eyes when I saw Reginald standing before me. His expression told me he'd been humbled. He looked almost pathetic.

I came around and grasped his hand. Even feeling like I was going too far, I pushed ahead. I disliked this man, but in his grief, he reached out to me. I had to help. "Reginald. I'm sorry about your mother. She was true Owens Valley royalty..."

He looked down his aquiline nose. "She was a dragon, a witch, and a..."

"Reginald, this isn't the time or place..."

He waved my protest away. "I've got bigger trouble than Mom kicking the bucket."

I pulled my hand away, appalled that he'd be so callous and selfish. "Reginald..."

"No, listen." His eyes scanned the room as it began to fill with customers. "Is there somewhere we can talk—privately?"

I certainly didn't want to be alone with him, but his desperation worried me. "Follow me." In the kitchen, I sent the two assistants to the front counter to help Emma. Libby was cleaning up. "Libby, can you wait in the office for me? We need to go over next week's orders. I won't be long here."

Thankfully, Libby was intuitive. She'd read between the lines and went upstairs. She slammed the office door closed. Her head poked over the stair railing. She wasn't going to leave me alone with Reginald.

"Sarah, I'm in trouble and need your help." He raised a hand at my imagined protest. I intended to listen to him, to see what he needed. Maybe I could help. He leaned on the worktable, sighing with frustration. "You heard all my employees bailed out on me this morning?"

"Yes, I heard."

"They said I'm impossible to work for. They're fools, and they don't understand business, but I must admit, the personnel part of owning Boulangerie has always given me trouble. I thought I could hire someone to deal with these morons."

"That's a promising idea, Reginald. What do you want from me?"

He took a deep breath as if diving into the deep end.

He squinted. "I thought you could help out as a manager until I get someone hired. That way, I could get my employees back to work."

"Me? What..."

He rushed over my protest. "It wouldn't be for long. It's only a half day in the mornings, and I promise I'll give you full rein. Please, you're so good with your people. They love you." He straightened at the admission. "I know because I asked around."

Stunned at his request, I considered the situation. Boulangerie was Layers' main competitor. But as I'd told him before, there was plenty of business for both bakeries. I worked at Layers all morning, and my hikes with Rusty in the afternoon had become such a delight that I hesitated to give them up. But maybe I could do both.

Layers was humming along nicely. Libby had blossomed into a leader as well as a baker. She'd volunteered to take on the apprentices next week and keep up with the baking. The two assistants, Marie and Charlie, were young and inexperienced. But both jumped into the job with an admirable willingness to learn.

The word had spread about Libby's success. She'd even signed up for college classes at the local Cerro Coso Community College for business management. Her enthusiasm was infectious, and I'd heard her telling her friends. I attributed her growing marketing skills to the rising number of high school applicants.

Emma had the coffee bar handled and, in my absence or during peak hours, Anna helped. Anna might be the answer. I knew she didn't want full-time work, but if I put a timeline on Reginald's bail-out job, she just might go for it.

"Reginald, I have an idea, but I have to hash out some

details first." I fished out a business card from my wallet. "Give me a call this evening, and I'll have something to tell you."

His eyes widened in surprise. I guess he'd expected me to turn him down flat. He nodded his thanks and left.

"Tsk-tsk," came from the top of the stairs. "I can't believe you. He confesses to killing your cousin, and you still help him out. He's our competition, for crying out loud."

"He's someone who needed help that I could render." I wondered at my own motive. Why help this evil man? "Besides, I'm not convinced he killed Melody."

Libby trotted down the stairs. "What do you mean? Of course, he did. He said so."

"I believe he was there, that he threatened Melody in some way. She backed up, tripped, and fell, probably hitting her head on a rock, just like he said. The fact that he didn't render aid makes him morally a killer, but that's not my judgment to make. I think someone was watching her, saw what happened, and after Reginald left, he took the opportunity to finish her off."

Libby tied her apron on and pulled a bucket of flour from the shelf. "You really believe there is a second killer?"

"I do." The hard part was coming up. "But no one knows who it is. It's unlikely that we'll ever know. So, we must live with it."

"You mean we have to live with a killer in our town? I don't like that one bit."

"Me neither."

Chapter Forty-Seven

That afternoon Rusty and I had just returned from our hike when Reginald called. I gave him the good news. "I have someone who can cover for me in the shop through next month, all of July. I'll need to do the books, so I'll check in at Layers every day. We have new apprentices starting on Monday, and I plan to be there in the morning, so I won't be at Boulangerie then."

He blew out a relieved sigh. "Thank you, Sarah. Thank you."

"How do you plan to get your employees back?"

He hesitated. "I've already called the lead workers and told them there will be a new manager—an interim until I can hire someone."

"Glad you asked me first." This wasn't going to be easy, but there was more at stake than to quit when the going got tough. I held the advantage, and I'd use it for leverage when and if I needed it.

"They were willing to come back to work if I stayed out of the way. They said they'd take care of calling everyone. They'll be in tomorrow at their usual times. I come... came in at ten."

"Ten?" Half the bakery's day was over by then. "I'll be in at seven." I wanted to see how the kitchen functioned. If it was as I expected, I wouldn't need to do much there. Boulangerie never had an issue producing bread and pastries.

"Thank you again, Sarah. This means so much to me and to the company."

I thought of all the employees who had walked off their jobs due to Reginald's mistreatment. I knew I'd made the right decision.

And the icing on the cake was I still had my time with Rusty. He'd have to stay at home, of course, but I'd pick him up on my way to the Buttermilks.

After dinner, I sat in the living room with Rusty snoozing at my feet. Dad was at a meeting, and Mom had gone out to dinner with her girlfriends. My life had been so busy lately that I felt soothed by Rusty's quiet snoring. I loved being around my parents but enjoyed my solitude too. This was one of those golden moments.

My phone vibrated. I was so content that I almost didn't look at the screen. Jake. I picked up immediately. He was another treasure.

"Hey, you."

"I was just thinking about you." That was true.

"Me too, so I called. How was your day?"

"Eventful. I'll fill you in after you tell me about yours."

"Got the test results back today. You're talking to Petaluma PD's newest lieutenant."

"Oh, congratulations." This was great news. He'd worked hard for the position and studied when he could. "I knew you'd do well. When do you start?"

"July first. I'll start on a swing shift, afternoons."

"What about Arco? Are you going to give him up?"

"We're in discussion about that. He's old enough that his retirement is on the books for next year. I'm arguing to keep him because it would take a long time for him to rebond with another handler."

"You must dread the loss of your partner." Remembering the loss of his wife four years ago made me regret what I'd said. Darn, I better watch it. "I hope negotiations go well."

"Me too. The other glitch in this deal is department doesn't want to pay a lieutenant to staff K-9 call-outs. I'm proposing a classification change where they pay me less."

"Less?"

"It's a reasonable way around keeping him and the department happy. It's not a financial sacrifice, believe me. My lieutenant's salary increase will make up for any call-out overtime."

"I'll keep my fingers crossed."

"I'd like to see you when I come down on Saturday. I'll be staying with Wesley."

"I'd like that. I work from six... oh, in all your excitement, I forgot to tell you my news."

I recounted Reginald's visit this morning and how I'd worked Layers's schedule to Boulangerie.

I barely got the story out when he interrupted. "You're working for Reginald? At his bakery?"

"Yes, like I said. He won't be there, or his people won't work. There's no danger for me."

"You're taking his word at face value. He's lied before. How can you trust him?"

"I don't trust him. The other employees will let me know if he shows up."

His voice low and gravelly, he said, "I don't like it."

"I knew you wouldn't." I tried a different tack. "The only reason forty-seven Boulangerie employees have their jobs today is because they won't have to work for him. They'll work for me."

"And you work for him." He snorted. "How long do you think he'll let you be the star?"

"It's only through July. He's already looking for a manager."

"I'll say it again—he's a liar. This could stretch on for months."

This was as close to a disagreement as we'd ever come. I appreciated that he wasn't telling me what to do. However, he gave me two cogent reasons to not work at Boulangerie.

"Jake, please trust that I know what I'm doing. And that it's for the best. Boulangerie is the second largest employer in Bishop. Closing the bakery would be a disaster for many families in this town."

"We won't agree on this. But my last word to you is—be careful."

"I will. And I'll see you Saturday. Text me when you get to Wesley's."

I felt strangely buoyed after I disconnected. I'd stood my ground in the face of Jake's opposition. I hated to compare him to Blaine, but they were the only men to whom I'd ever been close. I'd compromised or given in to Blaine more often than I'd cared to. He was a controlling manipulator, whereas Jake told me his reasons and let me decide.

I'd stood my ground and was proud of myself. Even if I agreed with Jake.

And Jake's promotion would make it likely that he'd

stay in Petaluma. He hadn't shown any inclination to move to Bishop—for any reason.

Suddenly I felt a tinge of sadness creep into my heart.

Chapter Forty-Eight

Thursday afternoon, I'd picked up Rusty, and we drove up Highway 168 to the Buttermilks. The day at Boulangerie had gone smoother than I expected. I spoke to as many employees as I could, one-on-one and in small groups. Getting an idea of what was wrong was important but learning about the strengths of the business was my focus. The staff and supervisors were knowledgeable and efficient. To a person, they loved their jobs. Even the custodians liked what they did.

What they didn't like were threats and intimidation. That was easy to figure. Mildred had kept the peace as much as possible, but with her death, staff saw their work lives becoming impossible. Javier, the lead supervisor, gave me a list of standards that Reginald had imposed months ago under his mother's radar. Many of the rules fed Reginald's micro-management style. He was interested in controlling the employees, whereas I wanted the employees to do their jobs. Javier and I sat down with most of the other supervisors and hashed out a basic list of procedures that met all the EDD mandates.

I'd recently taken an all-day seminar in human resource management for Layers and was able to apply what I'd learned to Boulangerie.

I walked away with the feeling that managing Boulangerie would be more about Reginald than his employees. Their dedication and work integrity were superb. He was lucky to have them. I hoped to help him see it.

But I had a trail to hike and an impatient pooch to liberate.

We drove the Buttermilk Road, a wide unpaved but graded road. In places, it was like a washboard. Again, I thought about selling my Camry and replacing it with a vehicle with a higher clearance. The Camry was great for LA freeways, but these mountain roads were something else entirely. I decided to put it off until after my stint at Boulangerie.

The afternoon was a full ten degrees cooler than Bishop with a light breeze. Clouds scudded across an azure sky like schooners sailing in the heavens. I wasn't the only one who enjoyed the Buttermilks. At a trail turnout, a red Chevy pickup and horse trailer sat waiting for their load to return. Near Loaf Boulder Road, a white pickup sat in a wide shoulder. We parked in another trail turnout on a Forest Service road. Rusty and I began our hike to the old pack station.

We'd made exploring the pack station a regular destination over the past week. Yesterday, we'd discovered a creek below the shacks. It had to be McGee Creek, according to my map. The pack station enclosures and buildings sat on a rock shelf that dropped down to the creek accessed by a steep path. Yesterday we discovered the trail from above when I had to call Rusty back from his adventuring. The sun was topping the mountains, ready for the Sierra sunset, so this exploration would have to wait for today.

Today, Rusty hadn't forgotten the promise of unexplored territory. He headed out at a trot as soon as he saw the pack station buildings. I walked between the buildings, following my canine guide. On the gently sloping path, I noticed two stubby pinon pines standing sentinel at opposite sides behind the buildings. Rusty broke into a lope uphill to the edge of the shelf. I saw him reach the trees, let out a yelp, and tumble head over tail out of sight. Scrabbling rocks and intermittent yelping indicated he'd fallen down the other side.

With Dad's warning in my ears, I ran up the slope, stopping at the trees. I looked down the hillside. Any hint of a trail was too steep to climb. If there had been a path, it was now a simple rockfall. Rusty found his footing on a sizable flat rock. He picked himself up, looking for me, then shook. I whistled to him. He put a paw on the rocky slide and tried to step up but slid back to the rock. He needed help.

I took a step but didn't get far. Something stopped my leg, preventing me from moving forward. The incredibility of it shocked me as much as Rusty's fall.

A faint disruption of the dirt caught my attention. I reached down, and my fingers found, then traced a monofilament line. I recognized it immediately as the same type of line my father used on his infrequent fishing trips.

Someone had strung this line from one tree to the other. At calf height, it was sure to trip whoever didn't see it.

This was no accident.

Chapter Forty-Nine

The rockfall had disintegrated the narrow path to the creek. Rusty sat on the flat rock off to one side, mouthing tiny whines. How was I going to get him out?

Jumper cables were the only thing I had in the car, and they couldn't help. I thought about the horse trailer. Feeling a little foolish, I shouted to Rusty, "Wait." He couldn't go anywhere but down. If he tried to move too much, that's exactly where he'd wind up.

Taking my pen knife from my backpack, I cut the monofilament line nearest to the tree on the left and wound it behind. I left my pack there and ran down to the Buttermilk Road.

I let out a whoop when I saw two horsewomen cooling off their mounts. I trotted the hundred-yard distance with emerging hope.

The women looked up, smiling as I barreled toward them. Even though the run had been downhill, I was breathless. One of them, a redhead with a white helmet, offered me water from a thermal water bottle. I took a deep drink.

"Thanks. Say, I need some help. My dog is trapped on a ledge just past the pack station. Will you help?" At their enthusiastic yes, I explained the situation.

The other lady was a tall, bronzed older lady who spoke with a faint German accent. "Cheryl," she spoke to her riding partner. "We need rope—how far down is he —" At my answer, she continued to Cheryl, "Grab two lassos from the tack box up front."

Then to me, "One length is twenty-five feet, the other is thirty. That should be enough."

The hike upslope was much tougher. I'd forgotten that the elevation difference could cause shortness of breath. It was the only warning I hadn't heard that night.

The women oohed and awed at the pack station but lost no time getting to the drop-off. Deciding to keep the information about the booby trap to myself, I pointed to the trees. We heard Rusty's faint whines as we stood beside a tree, surveying the situation.

The older woman, who said her name was Hilde, had explained on the way up that Cheryl was a volunteer fire-fighter. Her plan meant she would loop one end of the rope around her and rappel down to Rusty. She'd gather him up, and Hilde and I would pull them both up using the tree for an anchor.

It took almost an hour, and both Cheryl and Rusty were exhausted by the time Hilde and I pulled them over the ledge. Water from my thermos was warm from sitting in my backpack, but Rusty lapped it up. Hilde and Cheryl drank from another bottle, and then I drank. We sat in the dirt for ten minutes, catching our breath.

We'd all checked Rusty for injuries, and finding none, I pulled a leash out. I pointed to the hole at the boulder where Rusty had fallen through and warned them. They nodded gratefully, saying they'd be back to explore this place soon—with caution.

I managed my emotions until I said my final thanks and goodbyes to the horsewomen. Every minute that ticked by, I got angrier and angrier. This was intentional. Some person had wanted to injure another. Who and why?

Pulling out my phone, I took a picture of the two trees, the ledge, and the drop-off. I cut the loop of the monofilament line and tucked it in my jeans pocket. I had no idea if it would make any difference, but I planned to tell Kelly what had happened.

Chapter Fifty

Kelly was off duty that evening, so I gave my story to a deputy called Rangel. He'd come out to our house to see the photos and get the fishing line. I sent the photos to his phone and handed him the line, for all the good it would do. Rangel said unless there was a suspect, there wasn't much the sheriff's office could do. He'd notify the Forest Service as they managed land surrounding the area, but that would be the end of it. He tried to appear that he cared, but I never got the feeling.

Really, a booby trap, and no one cares?

Maybe I was overreacting. Understanding how law enforcement worked did little to diminish my wrath at the person who engineered this simple sabotage. He could have killed Rusty or me if I hadn't stopped when I did. Again, I blessed my dear father for taking the time to warn me of the dangers in the mountains. Not that he could've foreseen this threat.

Dad and Mom hovered in the kitchen while I spoke to Deputy Rangel. After he left—Mom hadn't even offered him coffee—I knew they were going to have their say. I sat at the kitchen table, Rusty snoring under my feet, and waited.

"Sarah," Dad began. "I'm glad my warning helped you be more alert today. But your mom and I are very worried about your safety."

"Mmm. Me too, *now*."

"We never thought that the oven falling from the stair landing was an accident. You said Kelly told you there weren't any fingerprints on it. That right there should've alerted you—and the sheriff's office. If you and Libby moved it upstairs, wouldn't your prints be on it? Somebody wiped the surface clean."

"You're right. I thought of that too. But I suppose I didn't want to believe that anyone would want to harm me." I rubbed my eyes. Fatigue was setting in. "Now I know better."

Mom elbowed Dad out of the way. "Look at you. You're exhausted. Are you hungry, honey?"

I shook my head.

She took me by the elbow and steered me to my room. "You need rest, maybe a good shower or bath, then bed." Rusty nosed the back of my knee. Mom said, "I'll take him out and bring him back. I expect to see you in your jammies by then."

When she returned with Rusty, I wasn't in my jammies. Fully clothed, I'd fallen in bed and was sound asleep.

The next morning, I counted seven texts from Jake and four voicemails. I didn't think he'd have heard about the booby trap already. Kelly might not even know yet. All amounted to the same message, *Call me, please.*

Though by the last voicemail, he'd dropped the 'please.'

I called him on the way to Boulangerie.

"I'm coming over now. I traded shifts, so I'll be there by two or three o'clock, depending on traffic on Highway 50. Tioga Pass isn't open yet, so I have to go Highway 88, to Carson City, and then to Highway 395."

Not sure about this change of plans, I asked, "What made you decide to leave today?"

"Don't act so innocent, Sarah." He didn't sound a bit angry. Worried, that was it. "Booby traps? When were you going to tell me?"

"How did you find out so soon?"

"Kelly called me as a courtesy. I asked him to keep me in the loop after the oven debacle." I heard Arco huffing and whining in the background.

"You're bringing Arco?" The thought of Arco and Rusty made me worry.

"Yes. He can hear your voice over the phone, and he's getting anxious."

That made me smile. "Will he be okay with Rusty?" I'd told him about getting custody of my own canine.

"He's generally good with other dogs. We'll go slow and take it easy. I'm hoping a simple introduction will lead to a lasting bond."

"Don't hurry. I won't be off until three or so. I'll be at Boulangerie most of the day."

"You doing okay after yesterday?"

"Yeah, just a bit tired."

"How about Rusty?"

"He seemed completely recovered. He's young and energetic." No ghosts of disasters that could've been to keep him awake. "He's fine. Hey, I'm pulling into work now. Gotta go. Text me when you get to Wesley's."

Chapter Fifty-One

Boulangerie was a delight. Where Layers was a challenge, having to set up almost from scratch since Melody's death, Boulangerie was a well-oiled machine. Tourists and locals returned with consistent hours, products, and service. The bakery had only shut down two days after Mildred Bateau's passing. The first closing was the walk-out, and the second was for her funeral.

The first few days went better than expected. Javier had things moving so smoothly that I wondered what Reginald could find that sent him into fits. I spoke to Reginald on the phone daily, thankful to limit our contact. Javier would work Friday, Saturday, and Sunday, so I'd have two full days off.

I pulled into the Layers parking lot just after two o'clock. I expected Jake to contact me anytime now, but I had to check in with Libby. She'd be cleaning up about now.

Layers' head baker rolled the last of the flour canisters against the wall and dusted off her hand with a flourish. The kitchen sparkled. Charlie put the baking trays on the shelves while Marie wiped down the counters. The bakers got a day off tomorrow, which was Saturday, so they baked double batches to keep pastries in the display counter. Coffee cakes were big sellers on Friday afternoons, and the line out front meant sales were going well.

Libby pulled off her apron and plopped down at the worktable. She and I had spent many hours there together. We'd grown closer than I thought was possible. She'd become the backbone of Layers and the inspiration for the nonprofit. She'd also become a treasured friend.

She pulled the hairnet off her head, and her hair stood out in spikes. Chuckling, I smoothed them out. She was so tired she didn't care, but she smiled her appreciation at me. I noticed her eyes were glassy. "What's the matter?" She hadn't heard about my close call yesterday, I was sure, not that it would make her cry.

"Next Thursday is the anniversary of my mom's death." Her chest heaved with a deep breath. "Ten years."

I slipped my arms around her shoulders, and she leaned into me. "Will you do something special to remember her?"

She pulled away and stared at the worktable. "Dad will be home, so no."

"Oh."

My silence always was the way to get her talking. "He doesn't do anything or say anything about that day. She literally was here one day and gone the next. He just keeps ignoring her like he did when she was alive."

"I'm so sorry you have to deal with this."

Libby straightened and met my gaze. "He's awful to be around. He's like, angry all the time, defensive. I don't talk to him. I'm afraid he'll take what I say the wrong way, and we'll get into an argument." Then, in a whisper, with her head bowed. "I hate it. I hate him."

I knew better than to tell her what to do. She was eighteen and would have to figure out how to manage her relationship with her father. There was no 'one size fits all' advice. She was on her own, but she had me.

"I can't give you any answers, but I'm here for you."

Her sad gaze fell on me as she squeezed out a smile. She laid her hand on mine. It was a gesture I'd used with her many times.

My phone vibrated. A text from Jake telling me he was at Wesley's. Libby jumped up and, with a brave but false smile, said, "Go. I'll be back on Sunday morning. I'm looking forward to a day off."

Chapter Fifty-Two

I made a quick trip home to pick up Rusty and drove to Wilkerson. Driving the unpaved Wilkerson roads in my Camry cemented my decision about buying a four-wheel drive. Bishop sometimes got snow in the winter, and the county road departments were overwhelmed with plowing. Some of these roads were as rough as the Buttermilks. Besides, I wanted a place I could put Rusty beside the passenger seat. I had nose art all over the windows and interior.

I wasn't looking forward to this visit. I hadn't been in Melody's house since she died. I know Wesley wanted to go over what happened that night, but I wasn't eager to revisit the most horrible night of my life. Wesley believed reviewing the event might help us find another perspective in the hopes of finding who killed her. I had to agree.

Besides, I wanted to put my vague worries about Jake to rest. He'd admitted to being out in the desert looking for Arco. That would've been the same time Melody was assaulted, first threatened by Reginald, then killed by an unknown person. I'd have felt better with Kelly here. He could help with the timeline.

Jake had suggested introducing Arco and Rusty outside. The Charters' home was at the edge of the Wilkerson neighborhood. The home was shaded with a pair of cottonwood trees, the landscaping left wild with sagebrush and scrub. To the south and the west was desert. To the east, almost a city block away, was a neighbor. The rest of Wilkerson was to the north. Their house sat alone like an unsociable hermit, distant by choice.

Jake and Wesley met me out front. Jake threw a rubber bone-shaped toy which Arco retrieved, then he anxiously pranced around, expecting it to be thrown again. I'd brought one of Rusty's balls and had it in hand when I let him out of the car.

Jake and I threw the dog toys simultaneously in a parallel direction. Both launched themselves after their own toy, then met in the distance. After some serious sniffing, neither pooch found the other to be a threat. Wrestling and romping followed soon after. Both Jake and I sighed with relief. It couldn't have gone better.

I shaded my view from the sun and scanned the terrain from Wesley's front yard. "Jake, is this where Arco took off?" I pointed opposite where I'd found Melody and Arco.

He turned and looked off in the same direction as me. "Yeah. I think he must've seen a cottontail. They're thick around here, and he's never seen one before. He was gone before I knew it."

"Okay, if I walk us through this scenario?" At Jake and Wesley's okay, I pictured the scene. "Dusk was approaching by 8:10, and suddenly Arco takes off into the desert in an unknown direction. Melody and Jake take off in opposite ways to find him. When did Reginald arrive?"

"He told Kelly he got there at 8:20 and left by 8:30."

All that damage in ten minutes. "Jake, did you hear the car?"

"No."

I continued, "Arco had obviously heard Melody trying to calm Reginald down. Animals are sensitive to human temperament, so he'd sense Reginald's anger. That he was protective of Melody spoke well of the dog's nature. So, he runs to Melody. At this point, Reginald has left, and someone else showed up, sees her in the sand, and goes to her." I mopped my forehead with a tissue. The day warmed up, predicted to be in the low nineties.

Jake took over. "Arco tries to protect her, but suspect number two hits him with a piece of wood. Runs him off so he can..."

Wesley stood suddenly and hurried away. Jake put a hand on my arm as I fought the impulse to follow him and offer comfort. This was important. I had to stay with Jake to get the full picture.

"And you came back when?"

He answered without hesitating. "Sixty minutes. I remember because I kept checking my phone for the time. I'm not familiar with how dark settles in here. I knew the sun would drop behind the mountains, so it would be sudden. Wes had told me I shouldn't go wandering after about 8:45 p.m., and I was already late." He kicked at the dirt with his heel. "The truth is I got a little lost."

This made sense. There were no lights except from the houses in Wilkerson. Out in the desert without a flashlight, a person could easily get disoriented. From this area, there was a small knoll which blocked the view of Highway 395.

"Okay," I began. "Let's pick up the scenario again. According to Kelly, Melody's time of assault was about 8:30 to 8:40, narrowed down between the coroner's estimate and my arrival at 8:50 p.m. She was over here, and you were up there? Toward the Apple Hill Ranch?"

"Yep. One of the farm workers hollered at me to go home." He laughed at the memory. "I had to ask him to point me in the right direction to get back. He must've thought I was a trespasser on the farm."

"Someone saw you?" Relief flooded through me. "Does Kelly know? I mean, that gives you an alibi."

"Yes, Kelly knows. He interviewed the guy the next day. Say, you put me on your suspect list?"

"No. I mean, *no*." Uh, yes, but I'm not giving that up. "But I'm sure glad you have an alibi. I wondered why Kelly didn't check into your activity." Suddenly it felt like a burden had lifted from my shoulders. I hadn't realized how much of a concern it had been. I knew he wasn't a killer.

Jake shook his head with a wry smile. "And still, you let me hang around you. You're not the Sensible Sarah that everyone says you are."

I managed to sound indignant. "I never thought you were a killer." Had I? I know I pushed his need for an alibi out of my head more than once. Was I denying common sense? It didn't matter. He had an alibi.

"Let's round up the boys and go inside. It's getting warm out here."

Jake whistled for Arco, and Rusty came scampering alongside his new buddy.

Inside the house, Wesley had used a swamp cooler to add moisture and cool the air. Familiar with my cousin's home, I went to the kitchen for tall glasses of iced tea for the three of us. The dogs lapped up water from Arco's bowl.

Settled into the sofa and chair in the living room, Wesley groaned. "Now what?"

Jake took a big swig. "Is it okay to talk about this in front of you? I mean, it's a sensitive situation, and if you don't want to listen, we can..."

Wesley picked at a fingernail. "No. You might need me to fill in your timeline."

"Okay, Sarah. Can you pick up the story?"

"I was northbound on Highway 395 just past the Ears, right about parallel to Wilkerson, when I saw him —Arco—in the road. At first, I thought I'd hit him. I stopped and realized I hadn't. But I'd seen the blood on his shoulder. I had to help him." I took a deep breath, recalling those excruciating moments. "I followed him uphill toward the houses. I found him out there." I pointed in the direction where Melody had been found, while watching Wesley. His eyes reddened. "The rest, you know."

Jake blew out the deep breath he'd been holding. "Wes, you were with Vernelle Kearney at her house, right?"

"She finally came through and changed her statement to Deputy McSorley." Wesley's voice was flat, like an automated recording.

"Okay, let's review Reg Bateau's statement." Jake knew how this should go. He was orderly and concise in the recap. "He says Melody was outside when he showed up. He started to yell at her about Layers, and she felt threatened. She backed up, fell, and hit her head on a rock. He said he panicked and left without checking on her. He was there ten minutes, tops."

Jake looked at us both and said, "What I don't get is, why didn't I hear his car?"

Wesley sat up, finally having something to offer. "Because it wasn't his car. It would've been his wife's car —and she's got an electric car. They don't make noise."

"Nice." Jake's head bobbed with satisfaction. "Thanks for that. I thought I was losing my hearing."

"Here's where the story gets murky." I began.

Jake took over, "Someone else shows up, sees Melody on the ground, incapacitated. According to the medical examiner, she was hit with a piece of wood at about the same spot as her original wound."

A thought struck me. "I know it won't help to iden-tify the killer, but the vet took wood splinters out of Arco's shoulder. He said he would keep them for evidence of a cruelty case." I shrugged at the triviality of it, but one never knows how important a sliver can be. "I'll call Kelly and tell him to get in touch with Doctor Vancleef at North Sierra Vet Clinic." Arco and Rusty had flopped on the cool tile floor for a nap. Rusty snored.

Wesley rubbed his eyes and stood. "I must go. I'm meeting one of the elders at church. Don't lock up if you leave."

Jake laughed as we got up to wash the glasses. "We have a running joke about life here in the Eastern Sierras. Where I live in Petaluma, everyone locks their doors at night. Here, no one does."

We stood at the sink, and I looked out over the desert, a dramatic landscape that always took my breath away. No wonder Wesley and Melody picked this house. "Yep, that's been a tough habit to give up. Mom and Dad are forever getting locked out of their own house. They've taken to carrying keys. Finally."

"Back to Wes—what he hasn't mentioned is the other thing I'm concerned about. You."

"Me?" Uh oh, I felt a lecture coming on.

"Yes. You're in danger. I don't think you can deny it after yesterday."

"I must admit that it shook me up. Rusty could've been hurt or killed."

"Listen," he turned to me, grabbing my shoulders to bring me around and face him. "As special as Rusty is, he can be replaced. You cannot. Please be careful."

"I have to live. I can't let some lunatic run my life with fear."

He let go of me and smiled. He pulled me to his chest, and I felt his heartbeat as he said, "There's no one in the world like you, Sarah." I rested there in complete security for a minute. Then, realizing how limited our futures were, I pulled away.

"So, what now, Lieutenant Charters? Do you have some great plan to flush out the killer? Some skilled insights into human behavior that will reveal him to us?"

"No plan other than to keep you alive. Suspect number two obviously thinks you know something that will give him away."

"I don't know anything." Anger welled up inside. Tears smarted in my eyes. I'd like to get this jerk and shake him until the truth fell out. "I've just told you everything. Did you discover any new clues? Do you know who killed Melody?"

"No."

I groaned. Jake must be terribly frustrated too. "What about being proactive?"

"You mean like setting a trap?"

"Why not?" I was clutching at straws.

"No way. Nuh-uh, Sarah. What or who—whoa, Sarah. You are not going to set a trap with you as bait. No way."

Arco stood up and stretched, eyeing his master. He'd reacted to the tension in Jake's voice.

I'd never noticed the little tic below Jake's eye when he got angry. I hadn't expected this level of protest. I hadn't thought the idea through at all. But maybe it wasn't half bad. I'd have to ponder it.

Chapter Fifty-Three

Saturday morning arrived with a promise. The sun rose in a cloudless sapphire sky. As always, the night air temperature cooled to the fifties, which signaled a ninety-degree day. Temperature swings usually swung forty degrees from the low to the daytime high. I hadn't yet acclimated to the cool mornings, so I took a sweatshirt along to meet Jake and Wesley at Mack's Pancake House on Main Street.

I'd slept in until seven o'clock, which meant I had to hustle to meet them on time. I'd taken the time for a quick shampoo and shower but didn't bother with a blow dryer. My hair was still damp when I met the two men on the sidewalk outside the restaurant. After hugs all around, I looked in the parking lot for Jake's white SUV to see if Arco was with him.

"I left him at home. It's gonna get too hot to keep him with me today, even with the AC on."

Rusty stayed at Mom's for the same reason. If we decided to do a road trip today where the temperature was manageable for the dogs, we'd go get them. Meanwhile, Arco enjoyed the cool tile and air conditioning at Wesley's house while the kitties hid on windowsills.

Twenty minutes later, Mack's breakfast dishes filled the whole corner table. Both Jake and Wesley had gone for a run earlier and were ravenous. Pancakes, eggs— scrambled and fried—with a side of biscuits and gravy sat before Jake, while Wesley had corned beef hash, also with a side of biscuits and gravy. I had a boring but satisfying veggie omelet with corn tortillas on the side.

Conversation was spun around Wesley's efforts to rebuild his church, leaving conversation about his struggles to make a life without Melody for another time. Jake talked about the natural wonders of the area. I found out he was relatively new to Bishop, having reestablished his relationship with his half-brother six years before. His visits were short with his three-day weekends, the drive —in good weather—taking up sixteen hours total. Jake still marveled at the jaw-dropping beauty in our backyards.

I made my decision about the destination for today. They'd left it up to me, and I had a place to show Jake that would knock his socks off. It would do Wesley good to get outdoors and stretch himself a bit. "I'd like to show you Lake Sabrina, Jake."

"I saw the name on a sign, but you're pronouncing it differently than I thought."

"That's right. You can always tell a local by how they say the name. It's Sabrina with a long *i*."

Wesley's face opened with a smile that I hadn't seen since I returned to Bishop. "There're kayak rentals at the café up there now. We could take them across the lake and hike up to the falls. And it's much cooler too."

Excitement rose in my chest as I thought about

showing Jake the beauty of Lake Sabrina. "It's like a piece of heaven here on earth. You'll love it."

The destination settled, Jake and Wesley drove to Wilkerson to pick up Arco. They would meet me at my house as it was on the way to Lake Sabrina.

Wesley called as I pulled into the U-shaped driveway. "I made the mistake of playing my voicemail. I wish I hadn't listened to the message. There's a problem at the church, and two of the elders are there now, waiting for me. I'm going to have to beg off."

A half-hour later, Jake knocked at the front door. Mom let him in and hollered, "Your young man is here." Delighted with the phrase 'your young man,' I ran to get Rusty's harness in the laundry room at the back of the house. As I snapped the harness on, I heard them chattering.

"Wes gets called out more than I do as a cop."

"He's completely committed to his vocation," Mom agreed. "It's not in his DNA to refuse anyone in need. He responds to every call for help, the dear man."

Thinking about Blaine's visits, I recalled my ex doing all the talking and Mom listening patiently. Blaine talked at people, not to them. It felt weird to hear Mom having a conversation with Jake. Not for the first time today, my heart thumped a little faster.

Rusty heard Jake's voice and wriggled loose from my hands. I followed him with an empty leash. "Looks like you have a fan." I said as my dog sniffed and licked, wagging his tail until I thought it might fall off. We'd been working on not jumping on people, and he'd learned the lesson well. I was pleased.

I clipped the leash on his harness and smiled. "Do you have sunblock?"

"SPF 50 all over."

"Bug spray?"

He patted the leg of his cargo pants. "In my pocket."

"Water, for you and Arco?"

Jake cocked his head and sighed. "This isn't my first rodeo, Sarah. I've been in the mountains before."

"Well, then, shall we go?"

Nineteen miles west of town, the road to Lake Sabrina rose to nine thousand feet in elevation. It was still early for tourists, but dozens of people walked the dam path, sat in the café, and stood in line to rent canoes, kayaks, and power boats. We parked in the lot, hooked up the dogs, and walked down to the water. The sun glittered on the lake like diamonds on velvet. The mountain air washed away any worries I had.

Jake blew out a stunned breath. "This is magnificent."

"Isn't it?"

"It amazes me that you'd leave this for LA."

"Me too." I thought about Blaine and how he'd made it a condition of our marriage that I'd move to LA. There hadn't been negotiation or compromise. I thought it might be different with Jake.

While I walked the dogs, Jake rented two kayaks with life preservers. I put the dogs back in Jake's SUV and met him at the marina.

I hadn't gotten into a kayak in several years, and it showed when I practically fell into the seat of a 'sit on top' craft. Jake was experienced, and it wasn't long before we were exploring the farthest shore of the lake. A short hike into the Inyo National Forest left us both breathless with the scenery and lack of oxygen. Back in our kayaks, we took our time paddling around the shoreline. By midafternoon, we reached the marina. The adventure had sharpened our appetites. Jake had worked off the big breakfast, and the thought of the berry pie at the café had me salivating. We sat outdoors with our dogs at our feet, enjoying our treats and two big cups of coffee.

"I hate to leave, it's so beautiful." He scanned the trees and the lake, then settled his gaze on me.

"I know. You should see it in the fall. The trees are breathtaking when they turn colors."

He lifted his arm to indicate the scenery. "This isn't the only reason I don't want to leave."

I nodded. "It's been a wonderful day, hasn't it?"

His expression slammed shut, like something had closed. "Let's walk these guys before we leave." We walked them along the road to the trailhead, almost a half mile away. Coming back, I noticed Rusty was still ready to run while Arco had slowed. We gave them water and loaded them into the back of the SUV.

It was time for this fairy-tale day to come to a close. Time to go home.

Chapter Fifty-Four

I had to pop my ears several times on the way down the road. It made conversation a challenge, but as we got closer to home, Jake swallowed. Capably negotiating the mountain road down to Bishop, he said, "When my wife died, I thought I'd never be able to feel love again."

Silent and waiting for him to continue, my heart thumped in my chest.

"Sarah, I like being with you. You're fun to be around. You're bright, insightful, and compassionate. No one could ask for more in a partner."

I waited, but he'd finished for the moment. "Jake, I enjoy our time together too. And I understand how you must've felt after your wife passed away." I summoned my courage to bare my soul. "Your wife loved you to the end. I didn't have that experience. I had lies and betrayal. It will take time for me to trust again."

"I guess we both have issues to work through." he said.

"We do." I took a deep breath, knowing I would push him away. "But we can be friends while we work on them, can't we? I mean, we are compatible. We like the same activities. We have a common background. Yes, you're a cop, and I'm a court reporter, but our differences are our strengths. We have a lot to build on, Jake. I'd like to start with friendship."

Jake pulled up in front of my house. Growing dusky, the lights were on in the front. I noticed lights on in Libby's house. I wanted him to say that we could be friends. That we'd help each other through our struggles. I wasn't prepared for what he *did* say.

With a sigh of resignation, he said, "Okay, I get it. You're not ready." He shut off the engine and turned to me. His brows drew together, and in his eyes, a glimmer of extraordinary strength of character shone through. "But I am, and I'll wait for you."

I thought for a second. "Does that make us friends again?"

"Yes, yes," he laughed. "Of course."

"Good, because our dogs have become fast friends." I got out and opened the back hatch. Arco sat up attentively while Rusty whooshed past me and trotted into the yard. At the front door of the house, I leaned into a hug. "You'll be spending the day with Wesley before you leave tomorrow?"

"Yeah. Church, then home to go through some of Melody's things. I don't want him to be alone for that."

I patted his chest. "You're a good man, Jake Charters." And I'm a fool to let you walk away.

Chapter Fifty-Five

It was Monday morning at Boulangerie, nearing eight o'clock, when Reginald Bateau made an appearance. Surprised employees shot narrowed glances at him, waiting for his usual unpleasantness. He ignored them and corralled me in the kitchen. "I want a report. How's this place working?"

A little irritated he'd showed up without the courtesy of a phone call beforehand, I said, "Let's go up to the office. I have some ideas and plenty to tell you."

"You can tell me here." He finally glanced around with surprise as if he expected to see chaos in the kitchen. To their credit, the bakers were all working and pretending to ignore their irritable boss. "Tell me in front of these ungrateful slobs who protest when I'm around. I'd like them to see the disruption it causes in *my* life."

"No, Reginald. Upstairs, in your office." I marched past him and made my way up to the office, feeling the stares of the employees at my back. I heard Reginald's heavy tread behind me. My chest felt tight, and I hoped an employee would warn me if Reginald was going to stab me in the back. Literally and figuratively.

Maybe *he* was the one trying to harm me. It wasn't out of the question.

He didn't wait for the door of the cluttered office to slam before he started yelling. Even overweight as he was, he certainly had superior lung capacity. "What do you think you're playing at? Trying to make me look bad, eh?" No wonder Melody felt threatened.

"What are you talking about?"

"I hear the rumors. I hear what people are saying about me, and about you. Like you're running a popularity contest and not a business. I want the account books. Give them to me. We can't be making money." He glared at an open ledger book on the desk.

I slammed the book shut and handed it over. It was his, after all. "What makes you think we're not making money? We've increased sales every day in the past two weeks."

He squinted at me, his lips thinning with distrust. "I don't believe you. It's easy to cook the books." He flipped through the pages so fast; I couldn't believe he saw any of the figures.

"Then don't take my word for it. Look at the bank deposits." I crossed my arms across my chest. He was really making me angry. I don't lie, much less cheat the books. He was here for another reason. I uncrossed my arms and leaned across his desk. "What's the real reason you're here?"

He stopped, threw the account book down, and turned away from me. "I've heard that people—my people—love you. They all want to work for you. They don't want me back."

I waved the idea away. "Reginald, I try to respect

people and treat them like human beings, not chess pieces. That's all I do. It's not magic or rocket science."

He twisted around to meet my gaze. "Are you saying I'm a bad boss?" His face flushed. Another tirade was imminent.

"I don't have to say anything of the sort, Reginald. Your people did. That's why I'm here."

That stopped him. His face drained, and he dropped to a chair.

"Now that you've settled down, I have some things to tell you. I found the perfect manager for this place." I sat at the desk across from him.

"What?" His disbelieving eyes blinked repeatedly. "I'm the one looking for a manager, not you. And, I haven't found anyone willing to move here. So, I expect you'll continue here through August."

I softened my voice. I knew this would be difficult, but I felt this was the answer to his problem. "Your guy is right here. Javier. He's your lead supervisor now."

"Javier? But..."

"No buts, Reginald. Your people love him. They're working for him, not me. He knows this business inside and out, has a good grasp of accounting, and gets this staff to work—really work—without drama."

"But he doesn't have college..."

"I know. I've been talking to him about picking up some accounting and business management classes at Cerro Coso. Most of which he can do online. He's willing, but I suggest you pay his tuition."

"Javier?"

I sat back as the idea sunk into his thick French skull.

He shot to his feet. "Not a chance. You're doing this to make me look bad. Now Javier thinks he can replace me, eh? I'll fire him first." Reginald's eyes lost all focus.

He saw something no one else could see. "And you! You're done."

"Right you are, Reginald. I'm done."

"You think you're so smart," he sneered. "I've heard all the plans you have for your little bakery. And you better watch them closely because they're going away. Soon."

"What do you mean?"

"I mean, you mess with the Bateau family, and you get nothing but trouble. Your little enterprise is on its last legs. You'll be out of a job by the time I'm finished with you. Let's see. Shall I start with the county health department?" He tapped his chin in a comedic expression of thoughtfulness.

I shook my head. I had nothing to fear from city or county agencies. He was full of threats and hot air.

"Reginald, you're right about one thing. I am done with you. I gave you suggestions, and you do with them what you will. I'm done."

I slammed the door, marched down the stairs, and felt the eyes of many staff members on me. I also felt sorrow at leaving these lovely people. What a treasure Reginald had—and ignored.

Chapter Fifty-Six

It was early, and I didn't want to go to Layers yet. They had the operation well in hand, and I had matters to think over.

Boulangerie was in my rearview mirror as much as Blaine was. I'd put all the energy I could into Reginald's bakery and made it a better place to work. It was his business to run into the ground if he wanted. I was just sorry for all his employees who had come to work every day, doing their best.

Blaine was also history. I couldn't change him any more than I could change the weather. I had no idea if he understood fidelity—ever. But at that moment, I knew I'd never wonder about it again. I only hoped I could stop comparing Blaine with others, specifically Jake, who always came out on top.

Driving aimlessly and unable to make any sense of my life, I found myself on the north end of town at Wesley's church. I drove by and saw his Toyota parked out front.

The late morning sun warmed my arms as I strolled,

casually, I hoped, into Wesley's office. "Are you free for a few minutes?"

"Sarah, come on in." He walked over to the door, closing it behind me. He leaned over for a hug and then pointed to a chair in front of his desk.

Noting the almost therapeutic atmosphere, I said, "You must do this a lot."

He sat, smiling. "I do. And it's one of the most satisfying parts of my job."

I glanced around the room, an unpretentious space filled with books of all types, a couch, and several amateurish paintings of local scenes. Wesley's desk sat off to one corner with the chair I sat in directly in front. It smelled like boot leather, a manly scent without artificial fragrance.

What was I doing? Confiding in the brother of 'my young man'? Suddenly embarrassed at putting him in the middle of my dilemma, I was at a loss for words.

"You're pretty brave coming over here. I mean, not many women would go to their admirer's brother to talk things over."

I couldn't take a deep breath. "Admirer? Did he say that?"

"Of course he did." His lips curled in a half smile. So like his brother. "He's crazy about you."

"Really?" This wasn't news to me. Jake had said as much Saturday. What stunned me was that he told Wesley about his feelings. I couldn't pry into specifics like I would've in junior high school, so I went on to the point of my visit.

"Then you know that I told him I wasn't ready for a new relationship."

Wesley nodded, clasping his hands together on the desk—a classic counselor posture. "I thought you already had a relationship. I mean, you two spend a lot of time together. You have mutual interests, not the least of which is your safety. You just don't want to take it to the next level."

"Yet."

"Yet? You already know him. I guarantee what you've seen is the real guy. There are no hidden agendas, no manipulations, no wild temper tantrums. He's as easy-going as you'll ever find."

I didn't need a hard sell. What I wanted was to fill in some of the blanks. No one knew Jake like Wesley. Jake had lived up north all his life and hadn't spent much time here. "Jake hasn't talked much about his wife..." Wesley winced at the mention. "...and I know she passed away four years ago from cancer. Did you know her?"

"I met her twice. Once before she was diagnosed, she and Jake came for a visit. Then, Melody and I went to Petaluma after her first operation. We stayed for a few days because Melody just took over meals and the household until her mother came in to help. But Kristin wasn't in any shape to be sociable."

"What was she like?" I hated myself for asking behind Jake's back. I should be asking him.

"When she was here, she was positive and helpful. She even cooked dinner one night. Good cook. They seemed good together. They didn't paw each other, but there was mutual respect and love too."

I pictured them, doing dishes, mowing the lawn, paying bills...doing all the activities that married people do. Well, most married people.

Wesley's brown eyes pierced mine. "Isn't that the kind of relationship you're looking for?"

Chapter Fifty-Seven

I arrived at Layers in time to watch Libby motor off on her scooter. When winter came—temperatures sometimes got down to freezing—we were going to look into getting her a proper car. Maybe talk Grant into freeing up Norrie's car, still parked in their garage. But for now, the scooter was a part of who my eccentric, talented, and very dear head baker was.

After saying hello to Anna and Emma, I headed upstairs. It was time to do the bookwork. This was the part of the job that I liked the least.

Then it struck me. Monday, our new apprentices had arrived this morning. Oh no. With the debacle at Boulangerie, I'd forgotten about them. I'd better call Libby to see what happened.

I rang and left a voicemail. She probably wasn't home yet, and answering the phone on a scooter was problematic. I'd started the second column of figures when my phone rang. Libby.

"Libby. I'm so sorry for leaving the apprentices to you this morning."

"Yeah, I heard about the mess at Boulangerie."

"You did?"

She laughed. "Yeah. We had about six of their employees come in and fill out applications to work here."

I closed my eyes. It would be all over town by now. News about Reginald was always juicy to the local gossips. I didn't want to think about it. "Did all the kids show up this morning?"

"Yeah. I'm not sure how well this will go, but I gave them a good pep talk, told them the rules, and issued them aprons and hairnets. They did all the paperwork that you set aside. Thank God you had that on your desk." I said a silent prayer of thanks for early preparation.

"Did you get enough baking done today?"

"Yeah. It was kind of funny, you know. Marie and Charlie pitched in like they owned the place. You know how good my scones are? Well, Charlie's are even better. You've never tasted anything so buttery."

"It sounds like today wasn't a complete disaster at Layers, anyway. They'll be back tomorrow?"

"Yep." I heard her smiling over the phone. "You know, I didn't mind being in charge. I kind of feel like I could really do this. I'm stoked about school this fall."

"That's great to hear, Libby." My preoccupation with my troubles had revealed a silver lining. I was so pleased that Melody's intuition, and mine, had been so right. "I'll see you tomorrow morning as usual."

We disconnected.

Chapter Fifty-Eight

"Sarah, Sarah." Anna's voice came from the Layers front counter downstairs. She sounded worried. Something was wrong.

Anna had walked into the kitchen, her eyes bugged out when I got downstairs. "Sarah, the building inspector is here, and he isn't happy."

I walked to the counter, and from the sour look on his face, it was clear he wasn't here for donuts. Tall with stooped shoulders, he reminded me of the cartoon version of Ichabod Crane. I wasn't expecting an inspector, but the landlord may have forgotten to tell me.

"Sir, can we step back here, please?" It was easy to see he was here for a complaint or something of that nature. News would travel fast about an unhappy building inspector at Layers. He followed me. As we passed through the kitchen, he stopped at the six-inch divot in the concrete left by the proofing oven. He took a photo with his phone and made a voice memo as I walked up the stairs. I couldn't hear what he said.

In the office, the man refused a chair. He identified

himself, "I'm Ed Strange from the county building department. I'm investigating a complaint about an unsafe structure."

"County? Unsafe...?" This building came under the purview of the City of Bishop, not Inyo County. And as for unsafe... that was ridiculous. "I'd like to see your credentials, sir."

As smooth as silk, he reached into his pocket and extracted a wallet. He flipped it open and held it up for me to see. Yes, the name was as he'd given, and he worked for the county building department. I searched for the date, but his thumb covered it.

"I can't see..."

"You've seen what you need to." He shoved his ID back in a pocket and inspected the ceiling. "Hmm. Drop ceiling tiles, two foot by four foot. What year was this building erected?"

Getting angrier by the minute, I leafed through the mortgage file and found what I was looking for. "Nineteen eighty."

"Probably have asbestos in them." He spoke to his voice recorder. "They'll need to be tested and probably replaced."

"Wait a minute." I stuck my nose under his. "I'm not the building owner. You need to take this up with him. And I'm quite sure you're not the right man for this job. Inyo County Building Department has no jurisdiction over the City of Bishop. How about I call the city right now to confirm my suspicions?"

Strange paled a shade and shook his head. "There's no need to do that, Ms. Murray." He backed away, looking downstairs at his escape route. "Sometimes our agencies help each other out when one gets bogged down."

"Mr. Strange, I suggest you leave. Fast now, before I call my friend, the deputy, and report someone impersonating a building inspector." The thumb that covered the date on his ID might reveal he was a former building inspector or retired. Either way, he wasn't who he said.

From the kitchen, I watched Strange hustle through the front counter area and bang the door closed.

Anna peeked around the corner. "What was that about?"

"Someone's idea of a practical joke."

Anna grimaced, "It sure wasn't funny."

"Nope." I had a thought. Anna and Tom knew a lot of south county folks, many in county government. "He said his name was Ed Strange. Do you happen to know anyone in the county government who might know him?"

Anna smiled broadly. "My nephew works down there at the county administrator's office. I haven't talked to him since Easter. I better give him a call."

I took over the counter while Anna did some detective work. Inside of five minutes, she was at my side. "You were right. Ed retired two years ago. He's not on the active roster." She gave me a satisfied smile.

"Did your nephew have any idea who'd put him up to this?" I thought I knew, but verified info held more weight.

"Did I tell you that Ed Strange's sister is married to Reginald Bateau?"

I couldn't get a clearer picture than that. Reginald worked fast. It had been a mere two hours since I'd left Boulangerie. Was this his parting shot, or was there more to come?

Chapter Fifty-Nine

Wednesday afternoon, I stayed at Layers, working on payroll. It was after two, and the shop was closed, everyone was gone for the day. With Rusty at my feet, I plodded through the software program that now compensated five employees, not including myself. Business was good. Next week, I'd add my name in the employee column.

My phone chimed an incoming call. It was Libby.

"Are you at the shop?"

"Yes, doing payroll."

"Can I come down and talk?"

"Of course. I'll put the kettle on for tea." Rusty was soundly asleep, so I left him in the office.

Libby arrived ten minutes later, hair wild from the scooter ride and face flushed. Looking closer, I saw her eyes were glassy with tears.

At the worktable, our safe place, she cupped her hands around the tea mug. Suddenly, she dropped her head to her chest. She sobbed. At a loss to console her, I stood beside her with a hand on her shoulder. If she wanted a hug, it was waiting for her. If she didn't, I wouldn't impose.

When her sobs abated, she sniffled. "I don't know what to do. Who do I talk to about this?" Her reddened eyes sought an answer from me.

I sat down beside her. "Tell me what it is, and we'll figure out who needs to know."

"Tomorrow, it will be ten years ago my mother died. I've been having these dreams about her. They're horrible. Horrible." She gripped her fists to her ears to block out the sound. "I can hear her scream over and over. A suicidal person doesn't scream when they're dying, do they?"

"I don't know for sure, but surely, at the last moment, they may regret what they've set in motion."

"I don't think my mother killed herself." She took a deep breath. There, it was out. This is what had been eating at her for almost ten years now. She'd been there that night according to what she'd told me before.

"They'd been arguing. That was nothing new. They argued all the time. It had gotten so bad that I shut it out. I quit listening. That night, I went into my room and played Pokémon." She faced me suddenly, her teeth chattering. "Do you think that if I'd stayed out there in the hall that she'd still be alive?"

The deep sorrow she must've felt made me want to cry. I tried to ease her mind. "I don't think anything you could've done would have changed the outcome."

"She called to me. I heard her call my name, and I didn't go to her."

"Was she calling you or saying something to your father about you?" Maybe I could lighten the burden by having her think about it in a different way.

She squinted at the memory. "I can't remember what she said. It's more of an impression. Let me think."

I poured her another cup of hot water and dipped a tea bag into her mug. She rubbed her eyes to massage the truth into view. "He was shaking her," she said, her eyes still closed. "He was yelling at her too."

"What did he say?" Dread spread through my chest. This felt ominous, like there wouldn't be a happy ending to Libby's story.

"He said, 'So what if I did it? I won't go down for it. You're going to take the rap.' What did he mean?"

Knowing a little about the circumstances around Norrie Armstrong's death, it sounded like Grant had been the embezzler, and he pinned it on his wife. But was there a more serious crime?

"Libby, how much do you know about what led up to your mother's death?"

With her eyes shut against the pain, she recalled. "I heard it at school, never at home. Dad wouldn't even say her name afterward. Did you know he keeps her car in the garage, after all these years?" She shook her head at the irony of it. "I heard there was an embezzlement, that Mom had taken money from the company. When the boss found out, she went home and committed suicide by throwing herself down the stairs."

"Maybe it's time for you to ask your father what happened." She might not like what she hears, but she deserves to know the truth.

"Yeah, maybe."

Libby gathered the dregs of her strength and trudged out the back door, like Marie Antoinette on her way to meet Monsieur Guillotine.

Chapter Sixty

I finished up the payroll and decided to call it a day. My phone read five o'clock, and the shadows of the Sierras were already creeping across the valley floor. Rusty hadn't been on a break for hours, so that was the first thing to do. Our outings to the Buttermilks were canceled for now, so I leashed him up and walked out the back door to the alley. I'd return to get my purse and lock up after Rusty's business was taken care of. Barricaded off from other parking areas, our small lot allowed for three cars and a scooter. The slots were filled when I arrived late in the morning, so I'd parked on South Warren Street behind the lot. After a few minutes, Rusty's activity was more sniffing than eliminating, so it was time to go back, get my purse, and lock up.

We had just entered the alley when I heard a car approaching, engine racing. I looked around but couldn't see any headlights. Momentarily disoriented, I stood in the middle of the alley, not believing that anyone would drive without headlights in the approaching darkness. A colored car whooshed toward me, veering at me at the last second. It wasn't white or black, but I couldn't tell what color it was. I yanked on Rusty's leash to pull him out of the way and felt metal slam into my hip. I whirled around and fell, letting go of the leash. The car looked like horns had sprouted on the roof. I hit the rough asphalt hard on the opposite hip.

Then, people yelling and Rusty howling reached my consciousness. I don't think I got knocked out, but I wasn't sure. Hands reached and grabbed me. I mumbled something about a dark car, and I heard someone calling for an ambulance. Lucky for me, the ambulance station was less than a block away.

I laid my head down on the gravelly asphalt. I didn't remember anything else.

Chapter Sixty-One

I woke up just as the ambulance arrived. I sputtered, beginning to refuse the transport, but both hips ached. The side that hit the asphalt ripped my jeans, so underneath was a nasty road rash. "Rusty? Where's my dog?"

A young woman, brown hair pulled back into a pony-tail, ripstop pants, and a sun shirt—a rock climber by the look of her, said, "He's right here. He's safe. I took your phone and called the person you set up in your contacts as In Case of Emergency, your mother, I think. Anyway, she's coming to pick him up."

I groaned, hating that Mom had been dragged into this but glad that she'd be able to take Rusty.

I spoke to a policeman in the blue uniform of a Bishop Police Officer but didn't have anything useful for his report. I couldn't remember a color other than a dark car, a sedan. No, I couldn't identify the driver. No, the headlights weren't on.

Hours later, my road rash had been irrigated and bandaged. Bruises, scratches, and a minor injury were a mere inconvenience. It could've been so much worse. An MRI showed no concussion, for which I was grateful. Mom had gone home and found a pair of pajama bottoms that wouldn't bind my wound and so I could go home without everyone seeing my hip.

Dad drove me home in his truck, the front seat being more comfortable than my Camry in my injured condition. Mom followed with Rusty in my Camry. It was almost three in the morning when I settled into my bed with several Tylenol on board.

Wesley was sitting in the living room when I awoke at ten in the morning. I hobbled out to greet him, Rusty at my side. According to my cousin, Dad was at the office, and Mom had gone to Layers to tell Libby, Anna, and the staff where I was.

Wesley guided me to a chair. "Rusty's already been out—several times. I think he likes the attention."

I scratched under my faithful mutt's ear. Wesley brought me a cup of coffee and a smile.

"It seems we're doing a lot of rallying as a family lately." Lame, but I couldn't think of anything else to say.

A rueful smile. "Best. Family. Ever."

I had to agree. My family had always been there for me. We had been there for each other. I thanked God again for Wesley, Mom and Dad, Anna, and Tom. I thought about how terrible it would be to have a man like Grant Armstrong as a father.

"Libby?"

"The girl from Layers? She's with your mom. You know she's well cared for."

But I was thinking more about what she found out from her father—if she'd asked him. I laid my head against the chair back. I'd call her this afternoon when she was done at the bakery, and the novelty of my hit-and-run had worn off.

Wesley cleared his throat. "I called Jake this morning."

"Oh no." I hated being the focus of so much attention. I knew I'd be seeing him sooner than later. "Is he coming down?"

Wesley's head bobbed a 'yes.' "I'm not sure when, but he's coming."

"You told him I'm okay?"

"Yeah, but he's coming anyway."

Chapter Sixty-Two

Jake wasn't due to arrive until lunchtime. When Mom came home at ten-thirty, she brought a visitor. Libby. Wesley left me in their capable hands.

I sat in Dad's recliner, an icepack on my hip. "You don't have to worry about me, Libby."

Her eyes held the sadness of the ages. "Yes, I do, Sarah. I've lost two of the most important women in my life. I'll be darned if I sit by and lose you too." She took my hand in an unusual display of affection. "You've become too important to me." She looked around the room at Mom. "I don't care if we have to stand guard over you twenty-four seven. Sign me up. I'll take a shift."

Mom's face was lined with strain. She'd been a rock through the past hours. This is what love looked like. The pain and the joy. "It won't come to that, Libby dear. There are people working on finding this jerk as we speak." I wondered who that meant? Kelly? While the incident hadn't occurred in his jurisdiction, he'd be poking his nose in Bishop PD's case. The PD had very little to go on, so I doubted there could be much to follow up.

Nevertheless, I wanted to reassure Libby that I wasn't in danger. "Are Marie and Charlie working?" Mom refreshed my coffee and put two pieces of toast on the end table nearby. I didn't have the heart to tell her I had no appetite.

Libby nodded. "Most of the baking is done, but I set them up with a plan for today. The apprentices are there to help."

"I hope to be in later today to meet them."

"They'll be gone by noon." She looked at her phone for the time. "You won't make it today. Tomorrow's fine."

I shook my head—slowly—at the inconvenience of last night's incident. Aside from a slight headache, bruises, and a sizable laceration, I'd not suffered any serious harm. Of course, there was the idea that someone wanted to hurt or kill me. The thought brought me up short. Libby and Mom's concern finally broke through the fog of my naiveté.

"Okay, okay. I get it." I closed my eyes, considering what this meant. What about Layers? The people around me—what about their safety? Now I worried about collateral damage. I pressed my fingers against my eyelids. What to do?

I decided to wait for Jake before I made any plans. I wasn't sure how sensible I was at the moment.

"Sarah, Libby said she has something she wants to talk to you about. Are you up for it?" Mom hovered over me. Her finger tipped up my chin, and she looked into my eyes, waiting for my answer.

I took her hand and squeezed. "I'm good." Without

smiling, she left the room, but I knew she'd be close by if I needed her.

"I need to talk to you about the night Mom died. I've remembered things…" Libby collected herself and looked at me, watching my reaction. "…Things that might mean something different than what we thought."

"Like what?"

"Mom pleaded with Dad. I heard her say, 'Don't do this. Think about Libby'."

"Do you think that's what you mistook for her calling for you?"

"Yes. Maybe. I don't know. But I did hear her say, 'Don't do this.' Sarah, I'm scared."

"What do you think it means?"

"I don't know. I'm not sure about the embezzling. I can't believe my mom would do that. Now, I can see Dad taking money that's not his. Even if he's just 'borrowing' it, it's wrong."

The theft was nothing compared to where my mind was going. Led by her breadcrumbs, I was following a trail that led to big trouble. I didn't know what to say.

"Sarah," she began. She'd already had this thought and was trying it on me. "Do you think Dad did the embezzling and Mom found out? When she wouldn't stand for it, he pushed her down the stairs?"

"You told me something of the sort on Wednesday when we talked." What was it he said? I remembered the three complete sentences. "'So what if I did it? I won't go down for it. You're going to take the rap'."

The living room suddenly chilled. I thought of how she must feel with the revelations. Her only parent alive was responsible for the death of her beloved mother.

It wasn't proof, of course. In a court of law, it's considered circumstantial, and while convictions occur, they aren't commonplace. The sheriff's death investigation was closed. This information might interest law enforcement but wouldn't result in a charge. Nothing would happen based on a recollection of a nine-year-old girl. Even if she heard what happened, it wasn't proof. "Did you ask your dad about it?"

With a sigh of frustration, she said, "He blew me off. Wouldn't even talk about it."

That could mean many things. He was full of remorse over pushing his wife down the stairs, or he is still grieving and couldn't talk about it, or despondent over her betrayal of trust, or he couldn't face she'd killed herself.

No proof.

"I have an idea. My friend, Deputy Kelly McSorley, comes on duty at four o'clock. Why don't you run this by him and see what he says?"

Finally, having a plan seemed to help Libby when she left. Even if it was tenuous, it was something.

Chapter Sixty-Three

J ake and Arco arrived shortly after 12:30 p.m. I wondered how many times he broke the speed limit. After an energetic and slightly damp greeting to Rusty and me, Arco settled alongside the recliner. Jake leaned over and kissed me on the top of my head. "Sheesh, I can't leave you alone for a minute."

I didn't have the energy for repartee. "This wasn't my doing."

His indulgent smile told me he knew it.

Mom was inordinately happy to see him. She seemed relieved, like her daughter would finally have a body-guard. The thought made me laugh out loud. I watched her hug him and felt warmed by her enthusiasm. I liked him too.

"Have you eaten?"

"I grabbed a sandwich on the road."

"Can I get you a drink? Iced tea? Water?"

With Mom, it was always about food. Yes, she was a terrific cook, but it was a comfort for her as much as appetite satiety. She extended the comfort to others she cared about.

A glass of water in his hand, he and Mom moved the dogs and me to the sunroom in the back of the house. It was a screen-enclosed patio that offered the view of Brockmans Corner, a cattle lease of green pastures. The room was warm without air conditioning, but the breeze kept it fresh.

"Kelly will be here any minute. He's going to help. When he gets here, I want you to tell us everything. Don't skip anything, even if you think we already know it. We'll start from the beginning. Do you want a notepad to write this down?"

I waved away the need for notes. "But you already know most of this." I sounded whiny. "You were here for some of it."

"Sarah," he stopped. As if willing his patience to speak, he said, "We have to figure out who's got a stake in harming you. The cops don't have the interest level to pursue this. I do."

"Jake…"

Resigned to the help that I couldn't refuse, I sat back. Mom came in with an ice pack for my hip, lingered a minute, then left. She returned five minutes later with Kelly in tow. In jeans and a T-shirt, he looked no less imposing than he did in uniform. No doubt, he'd leave here to get ready to go to work.

She sounded cheery, but I knew better. "Here's your rescue squad, Sarah."

Both men had sweating glasses of ice water in their fists. Kelly swallowed his while Jake started the ball rolling. "What do we know? No assumptions or hypotheses, just the facts."

Kelly began. "Melody Charters was assaulted on

Wednesday, June 1, between 8:35 and 8:45 p.m. Pronounced dead at 9:30 p.m. at Northern Inyo Hospital."

They'd forgotten a small detail. "Don't forget that Arco was standing guard over her body. He almost didn't let me get hold of him. He was injured and growling. He saw her attacker." I had a thought. "He knows who hit Melody. You remember his reaction when you grabbed my arm in the sub? He growled. He knows who killed her."

"Good point," Jake nodded. "But we can't arrest whoever Arco growls at. It's not proof, but it could be an indicator point."

Kelly pulled out a notebook from his back pocket and continued, "Wesley Charters was arrested for 187 P.C. at the hospital by order of Sheriff Stan Dorsey."

Jake pulled out his notebook, thumbed through a few pages, and picked up the narrative. "I was in the area but was alibied by a farmhand at the Apple Valley Ranch." He glanced at me with that Charters half smile that I was growing so fond of. "Sarah and I identified two other possible suspects and interviewed Vernelle Kearney and Reginald Bateau. Kearney was crossed off when she alibied Wesley. Bateau admitted to being in the desert with Melody but says she fell."

My turn. "Cameron Scherwin was also at Melody's house earlier that evening." Kelly's eyebrow raised. It was news to him. "He's seeing someone his father, the police chief, doesn't approve of. He and his father had an argument, and Cameron went to Melody to help settle him down at 7:15. He swears she was alive when he left, and the timeline supports that. He said dispatch called him at 8:00 p.m. to round up some of his loose cattle. Frank Scherwin confirmed this. But being the skeptic I am, I called to confirm this. It's public information. The time of the call was as he said." Kelly scratched furiously on his notepad.

"On Friday, June 3, Wesley was released from jail due to lack of evidence." Jake leafed through his notes. "That's not relevant as suspect info, but it helps to have a timestamp on the events. Now, what about Grant Armstrong?"

My heart throbbed at the thought of my dear Libby—yes, she was my dear Libby—the thought of her father as a murderer trying to cover up his tracks. "Guys, I hate to think about this guy…"

Jake was all business. "What kind of vehicle does he drive? Kelly?"

"Dunno." Kelly shrugged and glanced at me.

I thought back to his driveway. "A white Ford pick-up." Oh no. "There was a white Ford pickup in the Buttermilks when that booby trap was set. It was so far off, I didn't consider it."

Playing the devil's advocate, Kelly said, "Every other truck in Bishop is a white Ford pickup. We need more than that to look closer at him."

Jake's lip curled. "No, we don't. That's the beauty of an off-the-books investigation. We can look at whoever we want. Right now, I want to look at Grant Armstrong."

"We're talking about two different incidents here, aren't we? Melody's murder and the attempts on my life. Grant isn't on the murder suspect list. Is he?"

Jake put his empty cup on a tray Mom brought out. He smiled a thank you and turned to Kelly and me. "I see it as possibly three incidents: Libby Armstrong's mother's death, Melody's, and the attempts on your life."

Kelly whistled. "You think they're related?"

"I do. I'm seeing Grant Armstrong as a stronger suspect because of his history with his wife."

The picture in my mind was cloudy. I needed more facts. "What could be the motive?"

Jake provided the clue. "Who are the two people closest to Libby?"

"Melody and me..." The thought gave me chills. Because Melody took Libby under her wing, Grant assumed Libby told her about that night. It wasn't much of a stretch to reach the conclusion. Same for me.

I had one more question. "Why not..." I had trouble getting the words out.

Jake saved me. "Why not kill Libby? Good question. He must love her or think if she dies, it will look too suspicious for him. Who knows?"

I exhaled the breath I'd been holding. "I'm glad that doesn't seem to be in his plans."

Kelly stood up, considering his watch. "I have to get home to change for work."

Jake squinted at the big man. "Any chance you can use DMV to run vehicle checks registered to Grant Armstrong? What I'm looking for is a sedan-type vehicle."

"Like the one that tried to run over Sarah?" He nodded his approval. "I'll let you know."

The room felt more spacious with Kelly gone. He'd filled it with the interest of a cop who wanted to do the right thing. I knew he was helping us because of our history. I was pleased that we'd rekindled our friendship.

I looked out on the meadow behind the house, heard the cattle lowing, and realized a sense of peace was within reach. The headache was gone. My hip still ached, but it helped having Jake here to move the investigation along. I had a strong feeling this would be over soon.

Chapter Sixty-Four

J ake didn't stay much longer. With Arco at his side, he talked to Mom in the living room for a few minutes. He returned to the sunroom to make sure I was comfortable and left. When the door closed behind him, sadness descended on me. I worried about Libby and her father. And Jake too. If Grant was the murderer, he'd already killed twice. He'd have nothing to lose by killing a third time.

Rusty's tail thumped energetically on the tile floor as I stood. I opened the sunroom door to let him out into the yard. I stretched my arms, then rotated my shoulders. Even in the ninety-degree heat, it felt good to move. So good that Rusty and I ventured to the end of our land. I stood at the irrigation canal that bordered the property between us and the cattle pasture. In the distance, a full acre away, was the Armstrong house. I glanced at my phone for the time, almost four o'clock, and figured Libby would be done at Layers two hours ago. Had she asked her father about that night?

It dawned on me what danger I might have put her

in. I couldn't run over and check on her. I couldn't run anywhere. Besides, what good would that do? Force Grant's hand? Make matters even worse?

I texted Libby, asking where she was. No answer. Then, a minute later, *Meet me at Layers.*

Are you okay? was my reply.

No answer.

I had to do something. Text Jake and Kelly? Why? I had no idea what was going on. I didn't want to be the girl who cried wolf. So, I got dressed, left Rusty in the living room, and hobbled to my car. As I drove down the driveway, I saw Mom in the rearview mirror, trying to flag me down. I didn't want to stop to explain, so I sent her a text saying I was going to Layers to check on Libby. She wouldn't know that Libby could be in danger, but this was an acceptable reason to leave. She would fuss about me not resting, but that couldn't be helped.

I turned left onto West Line Street and drove downtown.

Chapter Sixty-Five

I heard Libby's sobs before I unlocked the door. She'd be at the worktable. Her sanctuary place.

Inside, I limped across the kitchen to her. Relief that she was safe flooded through me. My arms went around her small shoulders, and she folded into me. She mumbled something I couldn't make out, but I stroked her hair and held her until she ran out of tears.

She finally pulled away, and, with short, uneven breaths, tried to tell me. "He did it. He... he... killed Melody and my mom."

"Libby, you can't be sure." Then, I thought she *might* know. "Did he tell you?"

She shook her head and pointed to an aluminum cart in the corner. A dried-up tree limb, six inches in diameter and a foot long, with deep-brown stains marked along half of one end.

I froze. This was the instrument that killed my cousin. The branch, like a million other tree branches decomposing in the wild, that killed Melody and hurt

Arco. But... how did she know this was the one? He hadn't told her. Did she presume?

"Libby, how do you know this is the same branch?"

When she calmed, her face was red and puffy. I looked for injuries but saw none. "I just know. There's blood all over it."

"Okay," I couldn't refute her argument. I needed facts. "Where did you find it?"

"In his toolbox, the one he keeps in his truck." She sniffled into a paper towel. "I didn't ask him about that night. I couldn't. I wanted to know, but I was afraid. You see, I think I saw him push my mother. I was afraid he did it."

Seeing it from her perspective, I understood. "Then you'd lose him forever."

She nodded. I thought about how they fought so often, and he'd emotionally walked away from her ten years ago. Even in the face of this drama and neglect, she loved her father.

"But I can't trust my memory." She dabbed at her eyes.

Kelly banged on the back door, shouting a warning. "Sheriff's office. Open the door."

I released Libby and shuffled to the door. By then, Jake was behind him. Arco barked furiously in the SUV.

"Some of my mother's handiwork, I'm sure." I smiled as both my protectors rushed into the room. There was no danger here, but I was still glad Mom had called in for reinforcements. We might've needed them. Jake took his post beside me. At his questioning glance, I nodded that I was okay.

Kelly handed Libby a stack of napkins. "What's going on, young lady?"

Libby looked at me, her eyes searching for reassurance that Kelly could be trusted.

I nodded. "Tell him, Libby."

She repeated all she'd told me—her memories, what she heard and saw that night. "I talked it over with Sarah, and she said I should ask him. I was gonna. I really was."

"But..." Kelly prompted her.

"I started snooping around. I looked in his truck, the bed, the cab, the glove box, and then in his toolbox. I didn't even know what to look for. That's where I found that." She pointed at the aluminum cart.

Kelly walked over and inspected the limb. "Holy smoke. There's blood on this. A lot of blood." He tossed Jake his keys. "In the trunk of my car, there's a box with evidence envelopes. Get me a big one and a marking pen."

Jake was gone and back in a minute. He handed over the evidence bag and, from a distance, inspected the branch. "Hope we can get some answers now."

Libby sniffled. She leaned over and whispered, "Do they think this is what killed Melody?"

I thought it did but didn't want to say it without being sure. "They'll have to test it."

"Or I could ask him, like you said." She picked up her phone.

Kelly sealed the envelope and added his initials on the flap. "Wait a minute. Don't do anything until..."

"He's on his way." Libby said, peering at her phone. She sounded strangely calm.

Kelly's forehead broke out in a sweat. "He can't come down here and..."

Jake's tone was persuasive. "Think about it, Kelly. If we're here and civilians ask questions, we're in the clear.

You'll have to admonish him if he says anything incriminating, but if you're not asking and he's volunteering, maybe he'll even give a spontaneous admission. You're in uniform, but we'll keep the door open so he knows he's free to leave. He won't be under arrest."

Kelly scratched his head and considered Jake's plan. I wondered at the wisdom of this approach. I'd seen court cases lost under circumstances like this. "I have an idea. Jake, get Arco and bring him here."

Jake took out a key fob and pressed it. I heard a car door open, his SUV, and the thump Arco's footpads made on the asphalt. The K-9 ran to Jake and, at a sharp command, sat alert.

We didn't have time to debate.

Chapter Sixty-Six

G rant rapped on the front door. Libby trotted to the front and signaled for him to come around back. I doubted Grant had been in the back of the bakery. To my knowledge, he'd never been here. But I was sure he could find his way. Two minutes later, he marched through the back door—which had been propped open.

Arco's low growl caught my attention. A ferocious bark erupted, then more. Jake snapped a command, and Arco sat, laser-focused on Grant. A middle-aged man, wiry, with a full head of salt-and-pepper hair, Grant's sunburned face held an expression like he'd just swallowed pickle juice. "What's that dog doing here? Take control of him."

Jake stood, watching, with Arco still growling beside him. Grant's gaze settled on Libby, then scanned the room. His daughter stood beside Jake and Arco, Kelly near the cart the limb was on, and me.

"What is this? Libby?"

All traces of tears were gone, her face pale now. She

lifted her chin and asked, "Did you push my mother down the stairs ten years ago?"

He sputtered, "What are you talking about? You're nuts..."

"Dad. Tell me the truth. Did you kill her?"

Grant pulled his attention away from this young woman who was his daughter. His eyes skimmed over the room, his eyes settling on me. "This is your doing, Sarah Murray. You never could mind your own business."

"Leave her alone!" Libby shouted. "Dad, tell me."

Grant raised his hands, trying to look and sound reasonable. "No, she tripped and fell. Like I told the sheriffs."

"That's a lie. I heard you. I heard her. And I saw you, Dad. I saw you arguing on the landing. Your hand was on the back of her shoulder. You pushed her."

Grant sighed. He was in a corner with no way out. "You don't know..."

"Dad, what about Melody?" Libby strode across the kitchen. She pointed at the limb on the cart. "Did you hit her with this?" Arco snuck out a bark. Jake hushed him.

"What?" Grant focused on the branch and then the dog. Seeing them both jerked him back to reality. "Where did you get this?" Arco growled, low and threatening, and kept growling. Jake stopped trying to hush him.

"Tell me!" Libby's shrill demand cut through the room. Kelly and Jake stood unmoving at the drama playing out in front of their eyes. "Tell me the truth."

Grant dropped to a stool, head in his hands. "I did it. Both of them."

Kelly rushed to Grant's side. "You have the right to remain silent..." reciting the Miranda rights as he lifted him to his feet. He clicked handcuffs on his wrists behind him.

"Libby, I'm sorry." His voice was soft and petulant. "I didn't know you saw it all. I'm sorry."

"He's only sorry he got caught." Libby held onto the arm I put around her. She was spent, utterly wretched with the loss of both parents and the manner of their absence from her life. We watched Kelly get ready to lead the downcast Grant out.

"One more thing," Jake began. "Are you the clown who hit my dog?" Jake started as I grabbed his arm to stop him from doing anything stupid.

Grant looked up. "The dog was guarding Melody. I knocked him to move him away. He ran off, then I..."

Kelly interrupted him. "You can tell the detectives all about it."

Chapter Sixty-Seven

It was after midnight when Kelly stopped by my parents' house. He'd texted me that the detectives had finished interviewing Grant. Since Kelly lived in Bishop, I asked him to drop by to fill us in on what happened. Mom was still up, doing some mending, and Dad nodded off in his recliner. Although I was tired, I was still amped up from the evening's developments. Jake sat on the sofa across from me, Arco under his feet and Rusty lying beside me.

Once again, Kelly filled the room. We all stood, welcoming the hero into our living room. He'd changed out of his uniform into jeans and a long-sleeved shirt. Mom went off to the kitchen, of course, getting a snack ready for him and drinks for us.

"No coffee, please," Kelly responded to her offer. "I'll never get to sleep. Some water or…"

Dad offered, "A beer?" I thought about how odd it must feel for my parents to be relating to my childhood friend as an adult. They didn't seem to have any trouble.

"That would be perfect."

"Meg," Dad shouted to Mom in the kitchen. "A beer for Kelly, please."

We all sat in the living room, everyone but Libby. She'd crashed on my bed after agreeing to stay with us when they took her father away. I wanted to keep an eye on her because of the emotional turmoil she'd endured over the past weeks, especially tonight. She hadn't put up any resistance to the suggestion. I was sure she was relieved not to have to stay in that house tonight. Tomorrow, well, we'd face that when it came.

Not waiting for Kelly to finish his sandwich, Jake prodded his counterpart. "Well, what did he say?"

"They booked him for two murder offenses. The three attempted murder charges are forthcoming, pending Sarah's statement about what happened in the Buttermilks." If Grant hadn't been a neighbor of many years and Libby's father, they would've high-fived. I was glad they had the good sense not to do it here. I'm not sure my parents would've appreciated their cop humor.

"First, he admitted to pushing Norrie down the stairs. That's murder right there. The detectives spent quite a bit of time on that one. Chief Scherwin handed over his case files on the embezzlement to see if they'd shed any light on his motive." To Mom and Dad, he said, "There's no statute of limitations on murder, so he'll go away for a long time."

My stomach was in knots, but I had to ask. "What happened with Melody?"

Kelly wiped a bit of mayonnaise off his thumb and said, "It was like we figured. He'd gone out to find out what Melody knew about Norrie's death. He figured Libby had told her what she knew. It seems Libby never told anyone about what happened until Melody befriended her. He figured Libby didn't trust anyone with the information. She had friends in school but no one special buddy. Anyway, he went to Wilkerson to talk to her that night and parked down the street."

"That might speak to premeditation." Jake interrupted.

"Yeah, it might. He said he'd gotten pretty worked up after a fight with Libby. When he walked up to the Charters' house, he saw Bateau running to his wife's car and leaving. He walked out in the direction he'd seen Bateau coming from and found Melody lying in the sand."

I steeled myself for the details to follow. I saw the same determination on Mom and Dad's faces. I was glad Libby was asleep. She didn't need to hear this.

"He thought she was dead at first, then she moaned. And just like the medical examiner theorized, he grabbed the nearest tree limb, rolled her over, and hit her twice."

"What about Arco? Wasn't he watching over her?"

Kelly nodded, finishing off the beer and smacking his lips. "He was. Arco bit him twice in the arm. Just like at K-9 training." He smiled through his fatigue. "You know that tree branch he used on Melody? He used it on Arco first. Lucky the dog ran off. He'd have killed Arco too. I got some good pictures of the bite marks. They're almost healed, but Arco did some damage to a bad guy."

Mom spoke up for the first time. "Too bad Arco couldn't run Grant off."

"Yes," Kelly addressed this to me. "But the evidence the vet took from Arco's shoulder wound will encourage Grant not to recant his confession. It's been sent off to the lab, but I expect when the results return, they'll be able to match the wood and the blood—both Melody's and Arco's. Keeping that wood splinter evidence was a good move on the vet's part."

"What about the attempted murder of Sarah?"

"He copped to it. Said he used his wife's old car for the hit-and-run in town. As for the Buttermilks incident, Sarah will have to go in tomorrow and give a statement. He said he set the fishing line up. He'd been watching Sarah and knew she'd be going to the pack station. It was reasonable to assume she'd make her way to the trail at the back of the station. He didn't count on Rusty hitting the line first. He'd even knocked a bunch of rocks loose on the trail to destabilize it. He also 'fessed up to pushing that proofing oven out of the office and trying to get Sarah with it. Said he used Libby's keys to get in. He knew Sarah would come back to check on things at the bakery before calling it a night."

Mom's hands folded into fists. "Insidious." she said, looking away as if to visualize her own revenge on the man who tried to kill her daughter.

"What will happen to Libby?" Dad sat upright in his recliner, his day almost done. And tomorrow was a workday. I loved that he cared about her.

"I've been thinking about that, Dad. I don't know if she has any relatives nearby who can step up to help. I do know we are here and have known her for most of her life. She and I will have to check for…"

"Wait," Jake said. "She's an adult. She doesn't need family to take care of her."

I smiled, feeling a bit indulgent to my new friend's naiveté. "Of course, she needs someone. We all do."

Chapter Sixty-Eight

Dad rose, extending a gracious hand to Mom. "On that note, we shall retire. Six o'clock isn't that far away." They left, Mom scooping up cups, napkins, and a plate.

The kitchen sink faucet was running when Kelly stood. "Time for me to go." We said our thank-yous and goodbyes all the way out to the driveway. Arco and Rusty did their business in separate bushes. Jake and I waved as Kelly drove off.

I leaned against Jake's chest against the chill of the night. "He's a good guy."

"Um hmm."

"Let's go back in. You're cold."

Inside, I swallowed a Tylenol and sat on the sofa.

"I'd like to talk about us." Jake said, settling in with that half smile again.

A thread of excitement, a shiver of dread? "Now?"

"I have to leave tomorrow." He looked at the mantle clock and corrected himself. "Today. I have to work tonight, swing shift."

"Do you really have time for this? I mean, when will you sleep?"

"Later." He waved the thought aside, then clasped my hand. "You know how much I think of you."

"Yes."

"I'd like to get to know 'us' better. You know, spend time together—not chasing bad guys."

"I'd like that. But how do you suppose we can get around this distance thing?"

Jake sat back into the sofa pillows. He pulled my arm, and I settled into his chest. "I'm not entirely sure yet. But I know my life is more colorful with you in it."

"Colorful? Have you been listening to Taylor Swift songs or something?"

He blinked as his sweet half-smile softened his face. "Funny." His sigh came from deep within. "I can't imagine life without you. But I know you want to take it slow. I think it's a good idea to take things slow—for both of us."

I grinned. "The distance should keep things from heating up, don't you think?"

"I must be honest. With this promotion to lieutenant, I'm hoping to build my creds. I would like to be a real leader someday. Chief, maybe. But that means staying in Petaluma."

"You'd make a terrific chief. You're a natural."

"Thanks for that."

"As for the future, let's let it happen. I can't rush into another romance, but having a solid relationship with you would make the segue easier."

"I'll be making trips to see Wesley more often, you can be sure."

"And I might even be persuaded to visit Petaluma someday soon. Are there any hotels there?"